Baby-sitters at Shadow Lake

Baby-sitters at Shadow Lake

Ann M. Martin

AN
APPLE
PAPERBACK

SCHOLASTIC INC.
New York Toronto London Auckland Sydney

Cover art by Hodges Soileau

Interior illustrations
by Angelo Tillery

ISBN 0-590-44962-1

12 11 10 9 8 7 6 5 4 3 2 1   2 3 4 5 6 7/9

Printed in the U.S.A.   40

First Scholastic printing, July 1992

For my friends
Gladys and Keisha

Baby-sitters at Shadow Lake

Faith Chambers
21 Nappanee Court
Harrisport, PA 00241

June 2

Dearest Watson,

I imagine you're wondering why you're receiving a letter from your old aunt when it isn't even Christmas! Don't worry. Uncle Pierson and I are fine. I hope you and your family are well, too. I would very much like to get to know Karen, Andrew, your new wife, and her children. Pierson and I want to see you, too. We want to see what that boy we remember has become.

As you may have guessed, I am writing this letter for a specific purpose. I would like to propose something to you, and I want you to feel free to say either yes or no. I don't want to pressure you in any way. Do you remember the cabin on Shadow Lake in Massachusetts?

You visited us there every summer from the year you were five until the year you turned twelve. That was a long time ago, but you did like our summer retreat, so I suspect you remember it. Pierson and I don't use it much anymore, although we are still quite fond of it and of the lake community.

Just now we are in the process of rewriting our wills, and we were wondering if you would like the cabin. We want to leave it to you, but only if you want it. Pierson and I are aware that a second home is a big responsibility. The cabin is still maintained by Mitch. (The caretaker. Do you remember him?) Even so, you would have to make decisions about the house from time to time, pay for repairs, and so forth. Pierson and I don't want to burden you with the house — but if you think you would enjoy it, then it will be yours.

May I make a suggestion?...

"Aunt Faith's suggestion," said Watson, my stepfather, "is that our family spend some time at the cabin this summer, to see how we like it, and to see if we might want it one day."

"All *right!*" I cried.

"Are we really going?" asked Charlie. (He's my oldest brother.)

"How come we never heard about this cabin before?" asked Sam. (He's my next oldest brother.)

"Why is it called *Shadow* Lake?" asked Karen. (She's my stepsister.) "That sounds spooky."

Watson had called a family meeting. It was a summery Friday evening, and my entire family had gathered in our backyard. Most of us were sitting on the grass. The others were sitting on lounge chairs.

My family is on the large side. Not size-wise, numbers-wise. There are ten of us: Mom; Watson; Nannie (Mom's mother); Charlie and Sam, who are seventeen and fifteen; my younger brother, David Michael, who's almost eight; Karen, who's seven; Andrew, my stepbrother, who's four; Emily Michelle, my adopted sister (she's two and a half, and she came from Vietnam); and me. I am Kristy

3

Thomas. My full name is Kristin Amanda Thomas. I'm thirteen, and I'm an eighth-grader at Stoneybrook Middle School here in Stoneybrook, Connecticut.

Watson tried to answer the questions we were throwing at him. "I don't know yet if we're going to Shadow Lake," he said to Charlie. "That's mostly why I called this meeting. To decide."

He turned to Karen. (Karen is his daughter from his first marriage. Karen and Andrew also live in Stoneybrook, but mostly with their mother. Every other weekend, and on some holidays and vacations they live with us, though. It is a good thing Watson's house is actually a mansion, with plenty of room for everyone.) "I'm not sure how Shadow Lake got its name, Karen," Watson continued. "But there's nothing scary about the place, so you don't have to worry."

"Where is Shadow Lake, honey?" asked my mother.

"In the mountains of western Massachusetts. One of the most beautiful places I've ever seen. Anyway, that's what I thought when I was twelve. I haven't been there since. Come to think of it, I haven't seen Aunt Faith and Uncle Pierson in almost twenty years. Not since I was a very young man."

"What's the cabin like?" Nannie wanted to know.

"It's like a house," answered Watson, smiling. "I mean, it's large. If I remember correctly, it must be able to sleep twenty-five people. Maybe more. Two of the bedrooms are like dorms. Wall-to-wall bunk beds. The cabin sits right on the shore of the lake. A porch runs all the way around the cabin, and the place is surrounded by trees. It's really something."

"Oh, Watson, *please*. You have to let your aunt and uncle leave the cabin to you!" I exclaimed.

Watson looked serious. "I don't know. It *is* a big responsibility. But a visit there might help make up my mind. How would you feel about spending two weeks at the cabin this summer? When Karen and Andrew can come with us?"

I don't think I need to tell you what we thought of that idea. My brothers and sisters and I cheered, and Karen raised her fists and hissed, "Yes!" Then she added, "Can we invite friends?"

"Friends?" repeated Watson. "I hadn't thought about that." He glanced at Mom, and they held a silent discussion with their eyes. "Sure. You can invite some friends," said Watson finally. "Within reason." (More cheering.) "Keep in mind, though, that taking this vacation does *not* mean we're taking the cabin" were Watson's last words at that fateful Friday family meeting.

Well, we would see about that, I thought. I was already thinking of ways to convince Watson to take the cabin. I was positive Shadow Lake was a wonderful place. So I decided to keep a diary of our trip. After the trip, I would give the diary to Watson to remind him of our fabulous vacation. And of how much we loved the cabin.

Kristy

Wednesday

Shadow Lake, here we come! In three days I will be standing on your shores, swimming in your water, diving off your docks.

Our trip is on. We will leave for the cabin on Saturday. I am totally excited. Thank you, Watson. Thank you, thank you, thank you! We are going to have an awesome time.

That was the first entry in my trip diary. I intended to sound as enthusiastic and as positive as possible. I also intended to ask my brothers and sisters and friends to write in the diary as well, so that Watson would know I wasn't the only one having fun at the cabin on Shadow Lake.

Wait till you hear who was coming along on our vacation. *Twenty* people. (And I thought my *family* was big.) David Michael, Karen, and I had invited ten friends among us. (Charlie and Sam weren't interested in asking friends. They just wanted to "scope out the chicks at the lake" — in Charlie's words. And concentrate on water sports. And Andrew and Emily are too little to invite friends. I mean, too young. Actually, I mean their friends are too young to come on a vacation with someone else's family.)

Anyway, Karen had invited her two best friends, Nancy Dawes and Hannie Papadakis. The girls are in the same class in school. They call themselves the Three Musketeers. David Michael had also invited two of his good friends, Nicky Pike and Linny Papadakis. (In case you're wondering, Linny is Hannie's older brother.) However, unlike the Three Musketeers, who are best friends, Linny and

Nicky barely knew each other at all before the trip.

Also in case you're wondering, yes I invited *six* friends to come on the trip to Shadow Lake. How did I get away with that? Well, my friends and I offered to baby-sit free of charge for the little kids, all eight of them, during the vacation. And Mom and Watson took us up on the offer. They know my friends and I are good sitters. After all, we run a business called the Baby-sitters Club.

"Okay, you guys. Let's have some order," I said. It was the Wednesday afternoon meeting of the Baby-sitters Club (or the BSC). It was also a summertime meeting. School had ended. We were a little giddy with excitement over the big stretch of warm weather and freedom that lay in front of us. Not to mention our trip.

The meeting, as usual, was held in Claudia Kishi's bedroom. Claud is the vice-president of the BSC. (I'm the president. That's why I get to call the meetings to order. One day, I may buy a gavel for this purpose. For the time being, I rely on my set of excellent lungs.)

The other people present at the meeting were Mary Anne Spier, Dawn Schafer, Stacey

McGill, Jessi Ramsey, Mallory Pike, Logan Bruno, and Shannon Kilbourne. Mary Anne is the club secretary and my oldest and best friend in the world, even though we are not much alike. I'm loud and love to talk. Mary Anne is quiet and shy. I'm awkward around boys (*most* boys, that is), while Mary Anne has a steady boyfriend — Logan!

Dawn Schafer is one of Mary Anne's two best friends (I'm the other, of course), as well as her stepsister. Mr. Spier married Mrs. Schafer not long ago. Dawn moved here from California in the middle of seventh grade. She's *wonderful* with kids.

Stacey McGill, club treasurer, is also new (sort of) in Stoneybrook. She moved here from New York City at the beginning of seventh grade. Like Dawn and me, she comes from a divorced family, only her mom hasn't gotten remarried yet. Stacey's best friend is Claud. The two of them are extremely flashy dressers. You'd never know they're the same age as Mary Anne and Dawn and I. They look years older.

On that particular day, Claud was wearing a pink tank top over a white tank top and a pair of neon pink-and-black bicycle shorts. Also, she was wearing three pairs of flop socks, arranged so that her ankles looked like multicolored ice cream cones. Her sneakers were Day-Glo yellow.

Stacey was wearing a simple (for her) outfit — black leggings, a long black T-shirt with brilliant starfish swooping across the front, black flop socks, and high-tops.

"Doesn't black absorb heat?" I asked Stacey. "Isn't that why people wear a lot of white in the summertime? Because it reflects the sunlight or something? You must be boiling."

"Yeah, but I *look* good," she replied, and everyone laughed. Sometimes Stacey says things like that just to annoy me, since I couldn't care less about clothes. Mostly, I wear old jeans and turtleneck shirts and stuff.

Claud unearthed a handful of candy bars and a box of Mallomars from this pile of junk in a corner of her room. Her room is usually a royal mess. (Even so, it's our club headquarters, since Claud is the only one of us with her own phone *and* her own phone number, which are valuable assets for our business.) Claud's room is messy for two reasons. One, she's a slob. (Well, she is.) Two, she's a pack rat. Claud is an excellent artist, and she stashes her supplies all over her room. Also, she's addicted to junk food and Nancy Drew mysteries. Since her parents don't approve of either habit, Claud hides treats and books everywhere. Then she forbids anyone in her family to help her clean her room. Her secrets are (fairly) safe.

Everybody dove for the junk food. Except for Dawn and Stacey. Dawn only eats healthy stuff. (She actually doesn't *like* candy.) And Stacey can't eat sugar because she has a disease called diabetes. She *has* to eat healthy stuff. But she'd love to pig out on candy sometimes. She's pretty good about her diet, though.

Jessi Ramsey is also careful about what she eats, but she does allow herself treats from time to time. (For instance, at the moment she was eating a Mallomar.) The reason she's careful about what she eats, despite the fact that she's thin with these loooong legs, is she's a dancer. A ballet dancer. And an awesome one. Practically professional. She even takes lessons at a special school in Stamford, which is the nearest big city to Stoneybrook.

Jessi's best friend is Mallory Pike, often called Mal. Mal has *seven* younger brothers and sisters. Three of them are identical triplets (boys). And another one is Nicky, my brother's friend, who would be going to Shadow Lake with us. Mal has reddish, very curly hair, and she wears braces and glasses. (At least the braces are the clear kind that don't show too much.) She wishes she would hurry and grow up. Mal and Jessi are younger than the other BSC members. Most of us are thirteen and in eighth grade. But they are eleven and in sixth grade at SMS. They are very good for each other. Jessi moved to Stoneybrook from New Jersey at a time when Mal needed a best friend. And of course Jessi just plain needed friends, since she was new in town. FYI (that stands for For Your Information), Jessi is black and Mal is white, but skin color doesn't matter to my friends and me. If someone was *purple* and friendly and a good sitter, we would probably like her, and maybe ask her to take on baby-sitting jobs sometimes.

That's what Logan and Shannon do, by the way. They are associate members of the BSC. Usually, they don't attend meetings. We just call them when we need them. But summertime had arrived and everyone was feeling a bit more relaxed.

In case you're confused, let me tell you how our club works. My friends and I (but not Logan and Shannon) meet three times a week to answer Claud's phone. Parents all over Stoneybrook know when we meet and they call us at those times to line us up for jobs. Have I mentioned that we are all (including Logan and Shannon) excellent baby-sitters?

Well, we are. (I don't mean to brag; this is the truth.) We've had quite a bit of experience, so parents like to hire us. And we love to be hired. We earn pretty much money, we get to spend time with kids, and we have fun.

It was about 5:45 on that Wednesday afternoon. Our meeting was half over. We had given more jobs than usual to Logan and Shannon. (I think I forgot to tell you that Shannon lives across the street from me in the neighborhood to which my family moved after Mom married Watson Brewer.) The reason we had given so much work to our associate club members was that the rest of us were leaving for Shadow Lake on Saturday, so we wouldn't be available for two weeks. Logan and Shannon would both be around for one more week, though. After that, Logan was going to baseball camp, and Shannon was going to the camp she always goes to, Camp Eerie, to be a CIT. (In case you don't know, a CIT is a Counselor in Training.)

Ring, ring!

Stacey reached around Claudia and grabbed for the phone. "Hello?" she said. "Baby-sitters Club. . . . Hi, Mr. Marshall, this is Stacey." She paused, listening to our client. When she hung up, she said, "The Marshalls need a sit-

15

ter for tomorrow afternoon. That's short notice. Who can take it, Mary Anne?"

Mary Anne, our secretary, looked at the appointment pages in our club record book. "Mal can," she said. Stacey called Mr. Marshall back to tell him to expect Mallory the next day.

"That may be my last sitting job until after we get back from Shadow Lake," said Mal, looking a little wistful.

"Kristy, why does the lake have that name?" Dawn asked me.

I shrugged. "I don't think Watson said."

"Well, I bet I'll find a mystery up there," she went on. Dawn likes mysteries as much as Claud does, only she doesn't stick to Nancy Drew. She likes all mysteries, especially ghost stories. I knew she was hoping to stumble into some haunting tale.

At six o'clock, I stretched and stood up. "Meeting adjourned," I announced. "See you guys again on Friday — our last meeting before vacation begins." And then, even though I love to work and to stay busy, I couldn't help singing, "V-A-C-A-T-I-O-N . . . in the summertime!"

CHAPTER 2

Dawn

Saturday

Well, now I know how truckers sometimes feel. Today we traveled to Shadow Lake. We traveled in a convoy. So many of us went that we had to take three cars. We tried to stick together on the highway. I wish we'd had CBs or walkie-talkies or something. That would have been way cool. We had fun anyway, though. I rode with Watson (I hope you don't mind that I call you that, sir), Stacey, and the Three Musketeers, who are Karen, Nancy, and Hannie.

Dawn

While Stacey taught the girls silly songs, I asked about Shadow Lake, hoping, of course, for some kind of mystery.

Once, the eighth-graders at SMS went on a field trip to Stamford. We left from the school parking lot and we rode in a line of buses carrying dozens of other students and teachers. On Saturday morning, Kristy's driveway looked a little like that parking lot. Watson's van was in the shop, so we needed *three* cars to transport everyone to Shadow Lake. Watson was driving his car, Kristy's mom was driving her car, and Nannie (everyone calls her that) was driving *her* car, which is named the Pink Clinker because it's sort of old, and *very* pink. Also, it's clinky.

Early on Saturday morning, my mom drove Mary Anne and me to Kristy's house. As we pulled into the drive, we saw those three cars. All their doors were wide open, and so were the trunks of the Pink Clinker and Watson's car. Kristy's mom's car, which is a station wagon, is equipped with a luggage rack. Mary Anne and I arrived just in time to hear Charlie Thomas say, "Oh, come on, Mom. We can fit these two suitcases in the rack."

18

"We could *fit* them in, but I think the roof of the car would collapse. I bet we've already piled two tons of stuff up there."

"Well, where else am I going to put them?"

"In the trunk of Watson's car?"

"It's stuffed."

"In the backseat of Watson's car?"

"Then there wouldn't be room for Karen. . . . Hey! Maybe that isn't a bad idea after all. Karen, you — "

"Daddy!" shrieked Karen. "Charlie's making me stay behind."

"Oh, I am not," muttered Charlie.

In case you couldn't tell, Karen is a little over-excitable.

Mary Anne took a look at the chaos and said, "There's still time to turn around. Want to go home, Dawn?"

"And miss this adventure? Not on your life."

My sister and I said good-bye to Mom, who drove off waving. Then we ran to Kristy. She greeted us with, "I hope you guys don't have much luggage. We practically need a *moving* van."

"*We* don't," I answered, "but what about everyone else? Are Nicky and Mal here? Or Jessi? Or Claud?"

"No. You guys are the first."

Dawn

Watson, Kristy's mom, and Charlie had to pack, unpack, and repack the cars twice before they could figure out how to jam in all the baggage and all the people — plus Boo-Boo and Shannon. Boo-Boo is Watson's ragged old tomcat, and Shannon is David Michael's puppy. She's a Bernese mountain dog. I mean, she will be one day. I'd had no idea that they were coming to the lake with us, but I was glad they were. At any rate, I was glad Shannon was. Boo-Boo doesn't give two hoots about most people.

"Is everybody comfortable?" asked Watson.

It was later in the morning, and Stacey and the Three Musketeers and I had piled into his car like clowns. (You know, those little circus cars? The teeny-tiny ones? Their doors open and around thirty clowns tumble out.) I wasn't *exactly* comfortable, but I was okay.

"Yes," I said.

"No!" cried Karen. "I am not comfortable, Daddy. Hannie and Nancy are squishing me back here."

"Pssst! Stacey! Pssst!" Sam was tapping at Stacey's window. He motioned for her to roll it down. When she did, he leaned in and whispered to her (not very quietly, obviously, since I could hear him), "You look ravishing this morning, dahling, simply ravishing."

Stacey didn't answer. She made a face at Sam and rolled up her window. Then she said to me, "He is such a *pest*. He's been bugging me ever since I got here. He's like one of those little fruit flies. He keeps hovering around me, getting in my face, and I can't seem to slap him away or anything. Maybe if I said, 'Shoo! Shoo, Sam!' "

I giggled. "Somehow I don't think that would work."

This is how we were seated in the car. Front seat: Watson, me in the middle, Stacey by the window. Backseat: Karen, Hannie, Nancy. Ideally, either Stacey or I should have sat in the back with two of the girls, but the Three Musketeers flat-out refused to be separated. I wasn't sure why. However, I took advantage of the situation to ask Watson about Shadow Lake.

"It's a lovely place," he said, and sighed. "At least it was the last time I saw it, which was years ago. I remember thinking I'd never seen a bluer sky or breathed crisper air or swum in a clearer lake."

We had driven out of Stoneybrook by this time, and were zipping along the highway, Kristy's mom behind our car, the Pink Clinker behind hers. Stacey had turned around and was teaching the Three Musketeers to sing a silly song about a cow knocking over a lantern in a barn and starting a fire that caused "a hot time in the old town." Watson said the old town was Chicago, but I don't know how he knew.

"Anyway," continued Watson, "wait till you see Shadow Lake. I remember I never wanted to leave at the end of my visits there. I would always be driven home in tears. There's so much to do. Swimming, hiking, boating. Oh, they used to put on a boat show. That was fun."

An hour and a half later, I knew everything about Shadow Lake — except whether I would find a mystery there.

"Hey! There's a sign that says Shadow Lake!" called Karen from the backseat. "We're there. We made it!"

"We're *almost* there," her father corrected her.

We turned onto a tree-lined road. The trees became woods, and then we were driving through a dark tunnel of leaves. In the distance, something glistened. It was Shadow Lake. We drove nearer to it, then turned left and drove alongside it. We passed boats in the lake, boats at a dock, a huge wooden structure ("That's the lodge," Watson announced), a row of smaller wooden buildings that looked like stores, and then we drove into woods again.

As we crept along, Watson kept saying things like, "Hmm. I wonder if that's old Mr. Beaden. No, he'd be dead by now," and, "I swear that looks just like Junie Drake. Well, a grown-up version of Junie Drake." A couple of times he waved to people. "See what a friendly little community this is?" he said to me.

A few minutes later, after a couple of wrong turns, Watson pulled to a stop before a rambling, one-level house. (It was *much* too big to be called a cabin.) The other cars parked behind us, their doors opened, and everyone tumbled out, including Shannon and Boo-Boo.

As Stacey stepped out of our car, Sam trotted up to her and said, "Amazing, dahling. You arrived unscathed. Welcome to Shadow Lake."

CHAPTER 3

Jessi

Saturday —

Ooh, what a place.
Shadow Lake is better
than camp, that's
for sure. The front
deck of the cabin
looks right out on
the lake, all sparkly
and shimmery,
especially when
the sunlight is
reflected from it
in certain ways.
Plus, there are
no counselors. Plus,
one of the activity
rooms at the
lodge has a ballet
barre so I can
practice. Plus, I

Jessi saw this gorgeous boy. I hate to say that, what with Quint waiting loyally for me in New York City, but it's the truth.

Oh, my goodness. I should have known that a cabin that could hold twenty people would actually be a good-sized house. Watson wasn't kidding when he said the place could sleep a lot of people. This is the floor plan of the cabin:

Each one of the big bedrooms holds six bunks, so right off the bat, twenty-four people

can sleep in those two rooms. The small bedrooms can sleep two people apiece. We would
not be crowded at all, I decided.

Everybody had raced into the cabin as soon
as Watson Brewer had unlocked the front
door. We stepped into a large room which was
the living and dining area in one.

"Gosh," I said, gazing around, "this is so
pretty. And it's so clean and tidy. Who keeps
it this way?"

"Mitch," replied Watson. "Mitch Conway.
He's the caretaker."

We were all *oohing* and *aahing*, except for
Andrew. He burst into tears.

"Andrew! What's the matter?" asked his
father.

"This is . . . this is *nice!*" was Andrew's
angry reply.

Watson looked confused. "Yes," he said
slowly.

"But you said we were going to live in some
old cabin! Where are the logs?"

"Oh, no!" exclaimed Kristy, trying not to
laugh. "Andrew, you thought we were going
to stay in a log cabin?"

"Yes. Like the one Abraham Lincoln lived
in. Karen showed me a picture in a book. I
want to see the holes in the walls and the
cooking pot in the fireplace." Andrew paused.

Then he added indignantly, "And log cabins do *not* have carpets on the floor."

Kristy managed to calm her little brother down by suggesting that the kids explore the cabin. So they did.

While Charlie and Sam helped the adults unpack the cars, the members of the BSC led the children around the house. We checked out those huge sleeping rooms first.

"This is the biggest bedroom I have ever seen," announced Kristy, who lives in the biggest *house* I have ever seen. "It *is* like a dormitory."

"We claim it for the boys!" cried David Michael.

"Yeah!" echoed Linny and Nicky.

"Why?" demanded Karen.

"We just do."

"No way. It's for the girls!"

"Before you get into a fight," I spoke up, "why don't we look around the house some more. Who knows what we'll find."

Well, what we found was the other dorm, which looked exactly like the first one — rows of bunks in a sparsely furnished but very pretty room. In both rooms were braided oval rugs, white bureaus, tables made of dark wood, and several windows that opened into the woods surrounding the cabin. At the foot of each bed lay a neatly folded patchwork quilt, probably hand-sewn.

Nevertheless, David Michael said, "The boys still claim that other room. You girls can sleep here."

Karen shrugged. "Okay," she said. "We like this room better anyway."

"Just a minute," I spoke up. "Excuse me. How many girls will be sleeping in here, and how many boys in there?"

Stacey counted heads. "Including Sam and Charlie," she answered, "six boys in there, and eleven girls in here."

Mallory cast a long-suffering glance in my direction. "Not fair," she said. "Each of the boys will have an entire *bunk* to himself, and the girls will be crammed in here, filling up all but one bed. I've shared a room for most of my life. And now . . ." She trailed off. Then she perked up. "Oh, well. It could be worse," she said.

"How?" asked Claud.

"We could have shared a room with the boys."

"Ew!" cried Karen, Hannie, Nancy, David Michael, Andrew, Linny, and Nicky in one voice.

Sam and Charlie had been hauling suitcases and bags from the car into the cabin, and sling-

29

ing them in the living room. Now we began lugging the things from the living room into the bedrooms. The little kids claimed beds for themselves. Luckily for me, the Three Musketeers wanted to sleep in top bunks. Emily Michelle was given a bottom bunk, of course, but I still wound up with another bottom bunk for myself. I don't *mind* a top bunk. I'd simply rather be closer to the floor.

"Okay, let's unpack," said Mary Anne when the suitcases had been sorted out. She opened the top drawer of one of the bureaus.

"Actually unpack?" asked Claud incredulously. "You mean, put things *away*? In *drawers*?"

"Well, what were you going to do with the stuff in your suitcase?"

"Leave it there."

"For how long?"

"Two weeks. Until we go home."

"It'll get all wrinkly and old-looking."

In the end we decided to give ourselves half an hour in which to see how much organizing we could do. Then we went outside.

"Going exploring!" Kristy yelled to her mother and Watson.

"Have fun," they replied. And Watson added, "All the fun things are in that direction." He pointed. Then he gave Kristy some

30

money and asked her to pick up a few items at the grocery store.

I went off with the Three Musketeers who wanted to walk along the shore of Shadow Lake. We started off slowly, just dawdling and enjoying ourselves, stopping to smell flowers or to search for the cause of some movement in the underbrush.

"This is the life," said Karen a moment later as we stood looking across the lake. "Hey, I see a huge bird. A big crow or something."

"I see a sailboat," said Nancy.

"I see fish jumping," said Hannie.

"I see a cute boy," I almost said. (I stopped myself just in time.) But I did see an awfully cute guy. He was swimming in the lake. A younger girl was with him. Strolling along a nearby dock were a man and a woman.

Son, daughter, father, mother, I thought.

The boy looked about my age. The girl looked about nine. They were dark-skinned like me, and they were wearing brilliantly patterned bathing suits. I think what I first liked about the boy was that he was so patient with his sister. (He was teaching her to float on her back.)

Where do they live? I wondered. And at that moment, the man left the dock, crossed the path that ran alongside the shore of the lake,

Jessi

and strode to a nearby cabin. He disappeared inside.

Neighbors. That cute guy and I were neighbors. Well, that was pretty exciting. Then I realized something. I had nearly forgotten about Quint. Quint is sort of my boyfriend. He lives in New York City, and he's a ballet dancer just like me. We have *so* much in common. We don't see each other often, but we write and we talk on the phone. Once, Quint visited my family in Stoneybrook. I had a feeling that Quint was not roaming around New York looking for cute girls, so why should I be watching this cute boy? On the other hand, what was so bad about just looking?

"Jessi?" said Nancy Dawes. "Are you coming?"

"Oh, yeah. Sorry." I ran to the girls who had darted ahead of me, looking impatient.

We stayed on the path for awhile — woods on our right, the lake on our left — and sure enough, we soon reached the "fun" places. After walking through the general store and the tiny post office, I said, "Do you want to look in the lodge? I think we're going to be eating there a lot. Dinners, anyway. Also, that's where dances and stuff are held."

We ambled inside. For such a plain-looking building, it certainly held a lot of interesting things. Like the dining room, which was enormous; an actual ballroom; a counter where Shadow Lake souvenirs were sold; a weights-and-workout room; and several activities rooms, one with a *barre*! I was thrilled. I could practice every morning. No, I *would* practice every morning. For once, I could take a vacation without getting out of shape. Mme Noelle (she's my ballet teacher) would be pleased. Possibly surprised.

On our way out of the lodge, the Three Musketeers stopped at the souvenir counter. They each bought a blue Shadow Lake baseball cap.

My vacation was looking good: happy kids, a *barre*, and a cute guy!

CHAPTER 4

Stacey

Today was one of my days off from sitting. But aside from swimming, I wasn't sure what to do with myself, since everything at the lake was new to me. Finally I hung around with Mary Anne, whose turn it was to musketeer-sit. The day turned out to be a lot of fun, despite a scare in the morning. And despite Sam. Watson, Sam is your stepson, so I don't want to say anything mean about him. But he IS being a pain. He keeps teasing me....

On Sunday morning I woke up in a bottom bunk bed in the girls' room. I sat up and almost creamed my head on the springs underneath the mattress of the top bunk, where Hannie Papadakis was sleeping.

"Yikes!" I whispered.

I tiptoed to a window and peered through the screen. (We had slept with the windows wide open since the cabin isn't air-conditioned.) Outside were trees, trees, trees. Their leaves were bright green and glistened from the shower we had had during the night. I could hear lots of sounds, but they weren't the kind I used to hear in New York. They were quiet, country sounds — a breeze rustling those green leaves, Shadow Lake lapping at its shores, lone birdsongs.

Nobody else seemed to be awake yet, so I returned to my bunk and got in bed again. I thought about the day before. I thought about the car trip and exploring the cabin, but what I mostly thought about was Sam. He pretty much only called me dahling. And he was always staring at me. And he said ridiculous things to me that made me blush.

Across the room, Claudia stirred. She rolled over and looked at me. "Oh. You're up," she said. Then she closed her eyes again.

Stacey

But she didn't go back to sleep. And everyone else woke up. That was because Karen Brewer suddenly shrieked, "Spider!"

"Where?" asked Mary Anne. "Where?"

In a flash, we were out of bed, putting on shoes. Nobody wanted to go barefoot in the presence of a spider.

"Oh, wait a sec," said Karen who had inched her way to the spot where she'd seen the spider. "False alarm. It's just a piece of lint. Never mind. You can all go to sleep again."

But of course after a scare like that, nobody even got in bed again, let alone went to sleep. Instead, we dressed for the day. For a hot, very casual day. Most of us just pulled on shorts and T-shirts. When we had finished washing our faces and brushing our hair (which, as you can imagine, took a considerable amount of time, with eleven girls sharing one bathroom), we stepped into the living room.

"Dahling, you look ravishing!" Sam cried, touching my hair. (I hadn't expected him to be up, but he was. Darn it.) He looked at my ratty old shorts and my wrinkled Hard Rock Cafe T-shirt. "And your ensemble is — "

"Ravishing?" suggested Karen.

"No. Ugly."

"Oh, shut up, Sam," I said. (But I went back to the dorm to change.)

At breakfast, Sam sat next to me and kept tweaking the ends of my permed hair. Tweak, tweak, tweak.

I was sitting directly across the table from Kristy and gave her pained looks, but she didn't notice.

Finally, Sam tweaked my hair once too often. Just as I was about to open my mouth and really let him have it, not caring that everyone would hear and I would be embarrassed, Kristy stood up.

"Okay, baby-sitting assignments," she announced. Kristy had been working out some system in which all the younger kids would be cared for at the lake, yet us BSC members would still have several days off apiece.

I wound up with one of my days off, and I knew just what I wanted to do with that free time. As soon as breakfast was over and the dishes had been washed, I changed into my bathing suit. Then I walked to the dock, arranged myself on a lounge chair, and prepared to soak up some rays. "Sun, do your stuff," I murmured.

I was answered with a wolf whistle.

Sam.

I sat up and stared down the length of the dock.

"Hey, good-lookin'," he said.

"Oh, shut up," I said (again).

I snapped the lawn chair closed, marched off the dock, past Sam, across the path, and back to the cabin. Sam was being a royal pain.

I changed into my clothes again.

Would Sam *never* leave me alone?

I tried to figure out what to do next. Everyone had gone off in different directions. I sort of wanted to explore the stores and look at the big boats at the main dock — but not by myself.

So I was just sitting on the porch of the cabin when I heard Mary Anne cry, "Karen? Nancy? Hannie? Where are you guys? . . . Karen?"

"Mary Anne?" I called.

"Yeah. Stacey, is that you?"

Mary Anne ran around a corner of the cabin.

"What's wrong?" I asked her.

"The girls are missing! Karen and her friends."

"Missing?" I repeated. And then I couldn't help adding, "Already?"

"Yes, already," said Mary Anne testily. "We were going to take a walk in the woods. We were right behind the cabin. I turned around for about two seconds because I thought I heard Shannon whining. Just two seconds. That was all. When I turned around again, the girls were gone. You know, I saw something like this on *True Life Mysteries* once. This little kid wandered off and he was never seen again. His mother had just turned her back for a *split* second — and her life was changed forever."

"Oh, for heaven's sake, Mary Anne," I said. "Have you looked for the girls yet? Have you even *looked*? I think you're hysterical."

"I am not hysterical! I'm just scared."

"Well, come on. I'll look with you. Let's start in back, where — "

"Where last I saw them," Mary Anne interrupted dramatically.

"Whatever."

We ran behind the cabin. "KAREN!" we shouted.

"Yeah?" Karen, Hannie, and Nancy emerged from the woods. They could not have been far away, since Karen answered so quickly.

"Where *were* you?" cried Mary Anne.

"In the woods," said Karen.

Mary Anne sighed. "Don't go away from me again," she said sternly, "unless you *tell* me where you're going first."

"Okay," the Three Musketeers replied solemnly.

We ate lunch at the lodge that day. (We'd eaten dinner there the night before.) We took up four tables. I sat with Claud, Jessi, and Emily Michelle. Claud and Jessi and I were supposed to be taking turns helping Emily with her lunch, but Jessi had zoned out on us. She kept staring into space. Or, no . . . she was staring at *something*. I followed the direction of her gaze and my eyes landed on a tall, dark-skinned, handsome boy across the room. He was seated with a younger girl and a couple, probably his family. Never once did he look in Jessi's direction, but I was pretty sure he was who she was looking at. Hmm. . . .

That afternoon I hung around with Dawn. She said she was solving a mystery.

"What mystery?" I asked. "We've been here for all of one day."

"Shadow Lake's mystery," she replied. "I *knew* I'd find one. People up here keep mentioning a mystery, an old mystery. But they don't say much about it. Then, of course, there's the Lake Monster."

"The *what?*" I shrieked.

"The Lake Monster. People have also been seeing this — this *mon*ster in the lake. It looks like the Loch Ness Monster. Like a sea monster."

"Oh, my lord," I murmured.

I had taken a vacation with lunatics.

Mary Anne

This has been the most
surprising vacation of my
life. It's fun, so far,
but these unusual things
keep happening. I guess
the most unusual is
that my own sister has
completely lost her head
and is busy MONSTER-hunting.
I am not joking. Also,
the Three Musketeers keep
vanishing. Also, Kristy
found a speedboat and
she's going to learn how
to operate it. Also...

"Ow!" cried Mallory. "Ow, ow, OW!"

"What on earth is the matter?" asked Dawn. My friends and I were walking back to the cabin after our lunch at the lodge. Watson and Kristy's mom and grandmother were ahead of us. The younger kids were surrounding us, and Sam and Charlie were ambling along behind.

"Yeah, what's wrong?" Jessi asked Mal.

"I'm being eaten alive!" she cried. "Honest. Last night I got five mosquito bites, and now these tiny little bugs are stinging me or something."

"What tiny little bugs?" asked Kristy.

"These," answered Mal. She pointed to a dot on her forearm. "That's one. Two more were there but I swatted them."

"I hope those tiny little bugs aren't deer ticks," I said. "They carry Lyme disease, you know."

"Tell me about it," said Stacey, who thought she'd had Lyme disease once when the seven of us were away at Camp Mohawk.

"Thank you, Miss Encyclopedia of Bad News," Kristy said to me. "Those dots are not deer ticks. They're only chiggers. . . . But chigger bites really hurt."

"Oh, goody. Something else to look forward to," said Mal.

"Well, I don't know why you're getting eaten up," spoke up Claudia. "Nothing's bitten *me* yet. I don't think I've even *seen* a mosquito."

"Me neither," said most of us.

"I'm surprised," said Sam from behind me. "I mean, I'm surprised Stacey hasn't been bitten. Mosquitos like sweet blood."

"Oh, barf," muttered Kristy, and added, "I guess you'd know, wouldn't you, Dracula?"

Sam laughed. "I am a man of many secrets."

"Man? You don't even shave yet," said Kristy.

"Knock it off, you two!" called Mrs. Brewer. (She didn't even turn around. I guess she has what Stacey calls Mother Radar.)

David Michael, jogging along next to me, let out a snort of laughter. Then he turned to Nicky and Linny and said, "What do you guys want to do this afternoon? Go swimming, maybe?"

"Nah, too cold," replied Linny, at the same time that Nicky exclaimed, "Yeah, go swimming! I want to dive off the dock."

Linny and Nicky looked at each other. "The water isn't cold," said Nicky. "I tested it this morning."

44

"So did I. It's freezing," Linny replied.

"Wimp," said Nicky.

I waited for Mrs. Brewer's Mother Radar to kick in. It didn't. But Mallory's Big Sister Radar did. "Nicky!" she exclaimed.

"I'm *sorry*."

"Say it like you mean it."

"I'm sorry, Linny." (Nicky shot a dirty look at his sister.)

"You two have been crabbing all day," observed Mal.

"All day yesterday, too," added Charlie, who had ridden in the Pink Clinker with them. "What's eating you guys?"

"Nothing," they answered.

"Mary Anne? Can *we* go swimming?" Karen asked me, speaking for the Three Musketeers. "Even if the water *is* cold, we don't care."

"No, *we* don't care," echoed Hannie.

"Traitor," whispered Linny to his younger sister.

Hannie stuck out her tongue.

"Hey! We are supposed to be on vacation," said Charlie. "I mean, we *are* on vacation. So you kids can start having fun any time now. I give you permission. Trust me, *every*one will be happier if you settle down."

"To answer your question, Karen," I said, "yes, we can go swimming."

"Yea!" she shrieked. "Let's go right now. We Musketeers are wearing our bathing suits under our clothes! We are ready for anything."

"Hold it!" I put my hand in the air. "Not yet. You just ate."

"Oh, bullfrogs," said Karen, which made everyone laugh.

An hour later, I was sitting on the end of our dock (well, not *our* dock, because it didn't belong to me at all, but you know what I mean) dangling my feet in Shadow Lake. Around me were Karen, Nancy, and Hannie. They were swimming like fish, jumping into the water from the dock, paddling around, clinging to the float that hovered nearby, diving under-water. The water wasn't very deep, but it was deep enough for the girls to perform some acrobatics. They decided to put on a circus.

"Come in the water, Mary Anne!" called Nancy. "We need a ringmaster."

"I better not," I called back. "I'll be your ringmaster from the dock. How's that?" I have a little problem with the sun. I have this in-credibly fair skin, and I never tan. The only thing that happens if I try to soak up some rays is that I burn and then peel, which is not particularly attractive. So I was dressed in my sun outfit: a long-sleeved shirt, jeans, sun-glasses, and a straw hat. I was covered with sunblock (just in case) and my nose was a white triangle, because it was gooed up with Noze-Coat.

Guess what. My outfit was *not* the weirdest one in sight. Mallory's was. When we had returned to the cabin after lunch she had decided to arm herself against the Shadow Lake insect population, so she was also wearing a long-sleeved shirt and jeans, and she had fashioned a headdress for herself by draping a dish towel over her head, and *then* putting on a baseball cap. Plus, she had sprayed herself with Bug-Off, so she didn't just look funny, she smelled funny, too.

Mal and Jessi were supervising Andrew and Emily who were trailing Kristy, who was trailing Dawn and Stacey on their monster hunt. I took my eyes off Karen and her friends long enough to glimpse Stacey, who was holding her hand to her forehead and gazing across the water.

"Yo!" shouted Stacey. "Look out there! In the middle of the lake."

"Yo?" repeated Mal.

"She's from New York," I heard Kristy say to Mal, who nodded knowingly.

"What do you see?" asked Dawn, instantly on the alert.

"A big dark shape."

"A *shadow!*" shrieked Dawn. "Shadow Lake is full of mysterious, unexplained shadows!" She shaded her eyes, too, and then said, sounding awed, "Oh, my lord. That's no shadow. That looks just like Nessie."

It was Stacey's turn to act surprised. "Nessie?"

"The Loch Ness Monster. That's her nickname."

"Nessie is a close, personal friend of yours?"

"*Stacey*. The Lake Monster is out there. I think that's a *little* more important than — "

"You goon!" cried Stacey. "There's nothing in the lake except the lake. And maybe some shadows. I was just teasing. I don't see anything."

"There's nothing in the lake," said Kristy, "except the lake . . . and this boat."

"What boat?" asked Jessi.

"There is too a monster in the lake," said Dawn.

"Show him to me," demanded Stacey.

"What boat?" asked Jessi again.

"He's right out there," said Dawn. "Just look. See that — that *thing?*"

"That boat?"

"No, it's a monster."

"Is that the boat you're talking about, Kristy?" Jessi wanted to know.

"It's a *mon*ster!" exclaimed Dawn.

Kristy looked totally frustrated. "Not *that* boat. And it *is* a boat, Dawn, not something alive. Anyway, I meant *this* boat." Kristy pointed under the dock. Sure enough, hugging the shore in the darkness under the planks was an outboard motorboat. A little speedboat. No one had noticed it until now.

In the excitement over the boat, everyone forgot about the Lake Monster for awhile. We gathered at the front of the dock and peered over the edge.

"Is it ours?" I wondered. "Does the boat go with the house?"

"Don't know," answered Kristy, "but I'll find out." She jumped in the water. (She was wearing her bathing suit.) We watched her make her way under the dock, then tug on a thick rope. Presently the boat came into view, and Kristy called, "It *must* belong to us! I mean, to Watson's aunt and uncle. It's called *Faith Pierson*. That's their first names combined."

"Awesome!" said David Michael. "Let's take a trip around the lake."

"How?" asked Kristy. "Do you know how to drive this thing? Because I don't. Not yet. But I bet Mitch or someone could teach me." Kristy was off and running. Literally. She found Watson. Then she found Mitch. When she returned to the dock, it was with the news that *Faith Pierson* was kept in good working order, and that Mitch could teach Kristy how to use the boat with just a few lessons.

"Can I learn to drive the boat, too?" asked David Michael.

"I doubt it," said Kristy. "You can ask Mom, but I bet she'll say no. I bet she and Watson will make up some kind of age rule."

Which was exactly what happened. Watson and Kristy's mother came to the dock and stood around with Mitch, looking at *Faith Pierson* and asking questions like how big is the motor. After a long time they decided that anyone over twelve could drive the boat *if* they took lessons from Mitch first, and that of course no one could even ride in the boat without a life preserver. Then they wandered off with Mitch who was going to show them where the life vests were kept.

"You know what would be cool?" said Kristy who was now sitting on the dock, just staring at the speedboat. "If we could take the boat out to that island" (Kristy pointed across Shadow Lake to a green lump in the distance) "and explore it. Maybe have a picnic or something."

"Are you crazy?" exclaimed Dawn. "Ex*plore*

it? The *island?* That thing surrounded by Shadow Lake? I bet the island is haunted. Not to mention we'd have to navigate past a lake monster to get to it."

"Um, excuse me," I said. I glanced around. Panic rose in my throat. "Excuse me, has anyone seen Karen or Nancy or Hannie recently? I think they're missing again."

CHAPTER 6

KAREN

SUNDAY

TODAY HANNIE AND NANCY AND I
FOUND A SECRET HOUSE AND A
SECRET GARDEN. THEY ARE IN THE
WOODS. NOBODY KNOWS ABOUT
THEM YET. WELL, THE BOYS DO
NOT KNOW ABOUT THEM. WE
ARE GOING TO FIX THEM UP. THEY
WILL BE OUR OWN PRIVATE HIDING
PLACES. WE ARE GOING TO MAKE
THE GARDEN BEAUTIFUL, JUST LIKE
MARY AND DICKON DO IN THE BOOK
THE SECRET GARDEN.

This morning, my friends and I found two secrets in the woods. The woods are right behind our cabin. We found the secret house and the secret garden while we were supposed to be taking a walk with Mary Anne who was our baby-sitter that day. Only she was not with us. Somehow she got lost from us. We were not scared, though.

I was the one who saw the house first. Okay, it was not exactly a house. It was more of a shed or a shack. And it was falling apart. But we could fix it up. It could be our beautiful hidden playhouse. Hannie and Nancy and I could go to it to escape from the boys. (David Michael and Nicky and Linny were being gigundo pests.) Plus, we could play house.

But we did not get to stay in the woods long that morning. We were called back to the cabin by Mary Anne and Stacey.

"Where *were* you?" Mary Anne cried.

We had just come out of the woods. But in case Mary Anne had not noticed, I said, "In the woods."

"Well, don't run off again without telling me where you are going."

"Okay," I answered. But I felt a knot in my tummy. That was because I was lying. I knew

KAREN

I would not tell anyone when us Three Musketeers were going to our secret place. If I did, then our place would not be secret.

That day we ate lunch at the Shadow Lake Lodge. The lodge is kind of like a restaurant and a store and a place to have fun, all at once. Actually, it is like a hotel, but without rooms to sleep in.

Anyway, I simply adore eating in big dining rooms. And the dining room at the lodge was enormous. It was as big as a school cafeteria. But it was much prettier. Also, I did not feel any tacky old gum wadded up under the chairs. And no food was stuck to the ceiling. I guess people do not have many food fights in the lodge dining room.

Hannie and Nancy and I ordered hamburgers and French fries for lunch. We felt very grown-up because Daddy let us sit at a table all by ourselves. We pretended we were Lovely Ladies, and we ate our hamburgers with our pinkies in the air. Also, we ate our fries with forks instead of with our fingers. We hoped everyone was watching us.

"This hamburger is scrumptious," said Nancy. "I must ask for the recipe."

"And these fries are delightful," added Hannie.

"Yes. Not too hot and not too cold," I said. "And not too greasy."

"Yoo-hoo! Lovely Ladies!" called David Michael from another table.

"What?" said Hannie.

"Ignore him!" I whispered loudly.

"Have a Lookie!" David Michael opened his mouth wide. It was full of chewed-up food. He closed his mouth and grinned.

"Ew," cried Hannie and Nancy.

"I told you to ignore him," I said.

So we did. It was the only way we could be true Lovely Ladies.

Guess what happened after lunch. Kristy found a boat. It was tied up right under our dock, and we did not even know it. It was named *Faith Pierson* and Mitch said he would teach Kristy how to drive it.

Finding the boat was fun, but my friends and I wanted to go back to our secret hiding place. We had been thinking about it ever since we had found it. While everyone was talking about *Faith Pierson*, we were talking about the secret house and the secret garden.

"We need some nails," Hannie whispered to me. "And a hammer. And some paper towels and stuff to clean with. And a rake for the garden."

"I know. We have a lot of work to do," I

replied. I looked around. Kristy and her friends were peering into the boat. So were Daddy and David Michael and the boys and everyone.

It was a good time to escape.

"Come on," I whispered to Hannie and Nancy. "Let's go."

We tiptoed off the dock. We snuck back to the cabin. No one was paying even a teensy bit of attention to us. So we raided the cabin. When our arms were full with cleaning things and tools and the rake, we darted into the woods. Once, I peeped over my shoulder. No one was behind us. I could not see *any*body. They were probably still on the dock. Perfect.

Nancy was the first one to reach our secret house. "You know who I feel like?" she asked. "Snow White, that's who. I feel like I've found this dirty old cottage in the woods and the dwarfs live here, only I don't know that because I haven't met them yet. And soon they will come back from the mines or wherever they work, and I will clean up their cottage for them."

"Cool," I said.

We began to work. First we swept out the shack. Dirt and dust blew all over the place. I watched it float out the door in the sunlight. Then we wiped off the table and chairs. The shack looked a *little* better. But it was not very cheerful. Mostly, it was brown.

"The windows need curtains," said Nancy.

"*Every*thing needs paint," said Hannie.

"Maybe the windows would look better if we washed them," I said. I began to wipe the glass with a square of paper towel. And what did I see when the first window pane was clean? A face. A face was looking in at me through the clean window. Its eyes stared right into my eyes.

I screamed.

The person behind the face screamed. Then a voice said, "Karen?"

"Mary Anne?" I replied.

The face left the window. Mary Anne appeared in the doorway. "Karen!" she cried. "Hannie! Nancy! What are you doing here? You ran off again. I *told* you not to go anywhere without telling me first."

"But this place is supposed to be a secret," I replied.

"Our secret house," added Nancy.

"And our secret garden," said Hannie, pointing outdoors.

"I don't care. You may not keep disappearing like this. I'm responsible for you," Mary Anne said. "And just this morning, Karen, you *pro*mised — "

"I know," I interrupted. "I'm sorry." I paused. Then I went on. "But we *do* have a reason for keeping secrets. Do you want to know what it is?"

Mary Anne nodded. She was still standing in the doorway, hands on hips.

"We don't want the boys to know about this house," I told her.

"The boys?"

"Well, really just David Michael and Nicky and Linny. They will want to play here, too. But *we* want to play house here."

"And fix up the garden," said Hannie.

"Like Mary and Dickon in *The Secret Garden*," I added.

Mary Anne smiled. "*The Secret Garden*," she repeated. "I love that book. I'll tell you what, you guys. Now that I've found your secret house and secret garden anyway, why don't I tell the grown-ups about it? Also Kristy and the rest of my friends, since they baby-sit for you, too. Then you tell one of us when you want to come play here by yourselves. But none of *us* will tell the boys. That way, we'll know where you are, but your secret will be safe from the boys."

I thought about Mary Anne's offer.

"Is that okay?" I whispered to Nancy and Hannie. They nodded. "All right," I said to

Mary Anne. "It's a deal. And, um, I really am sorry we ran away again. We did not mean to scare you."

Mary Anne let us play in the woods by ourselves then. After she left, the Three Musketeers took turns raking the garden. We pretended we were on the moors of England. We pretended we were waiting for Dickon to pay us a visit.

Kristy

Tuesday

Tonight my friends and I ate at the lodge BY OURSELVES. Everyone else stayed at the cabin because you were barbecuing dinner, Watson, but we wanted to feel grown-up and independent. Note that I did not say we wanted to feel well-dressed. Just adult. Oh, well. Eating at the lodge turned out to be really fun. We did feel adult. But some other important things happened, too. For one, I got another of my great ideas. I'm not sure everyone else thought it was so terrific, though. Dawn certainly didn't.

"Mom? What are you doing?" I asked. It was the middle of the afternoon. My mother was in the kitchen, barefoot, wearing only her bikini bathing suit and a long shirt which belonged to Watson. (I, for one, do *not* wear bikinis. I do not think anyone should, really, especially if they are past thirty. But, in all honesty, my mom looked pretty good — for an over-thirty mother. *Maybe* I will wear a bikini one day, but only after I actually have a chest. When you're as flat as I am, there is no sense in wearing a skimpy little top. Why should I, when I don't even need a bra yet? At the rate I'm growing, though, I probably won't *have* a chest until I'm, like, twenty-eight, and then there'll just be a measly two-year window of time in which to find and wear a bikini.)

Mom was opening and closing cupboard doors and scanning the contents of the refrigerator. "I thought we'd eat supper here tonight," she said.

"Not at the lodge?" We'd eaten lunch and dinner at the lodge every day since we'd arrived at Shadow Lake.

"We need a change. I'm a little too familiar with the menu at the lodge. Besides, Watson thought a barbecue would be fun."

63

I thought a barbecue would be fun, too. I thought eating at the lodge that night with just my friends would be even more fun. So did Mary Anne and Stacey and Jessi and Claud and Mal and especially Dawn, since she's a vegetarian and never fares very well at barbecues. What's she supposed to do? Grill lettuce?

So I asked Mom and Watson for permission to eat at the lodge instead of staying at home and joining in the barbecue. I kind of made Dawn's problem a little more dire than it really was, considering she *could* have eaten salad and corn-on-the-cob while the rest of us scarfed up meat.

At any rate, permission was granted. Late that afternoon, while Watson and Nannie piled charcoal briquettes into a pyramid in the grill, and Mom and David Michael began to concoct their "secret" barbecue sauce, the members of the BSC closed themselves into the girls' dorm.

"Why?" I asked.

"So we can get ready for dinner," replied Stacey. She might as well have said, "Where did you leave your brain, Kristy? In the lake?"

"What's to get ready? We can go as we are."

"I am not going anywhere with Mal," said Claudia, "until she gets rid of *that*."

Mallory's insect headdress had become more elaborate. She had found one of those heavy jungle safari hats in a closet, and she now wore it over the towel. Most embarrassing, though, was that she then draped mosquito netting over the hat so that it hung down, swathing her entire head.

Mal set her jaw. She didn't respond to Claudia, just continued buttoning the front of her yellow-flowered sundress.

"You guys, we *don't* have to get dressed-up," I said. I was wearing a pair of blue shorts that fastened with a drawstring, and a T-shirt with a picture of Gumby on the front and a picture of Pokey on the back. I was very comfortable. "Nobody gets dressed up to go to the lodge," I added.

"Nobody wears Gumby shirts to the lodge dining room, either," said Stace.

I gave in. My friends were changing into dresses or short skirts or Capri pants with loose, summery tops. Since I didn't want to stick out during dinner, I put on a dress, too. (It wasn't mine. I hadn't packed one. It belonged to Mary Anne and it was slightly too long, but so what.)

"Is everybody ready?" I asked finally.

"Yes," replied a chorus of voices.

"Almost," replied Mal.

We all looked at her. The towel was draped over her head. She was holding the safari hat in one hand and the mosquito netting in the other.

"Oh, no," exclaimed Claudia. "No way. You are not wearing that."

"Yes, I am. I'm wearing it to the lodge. And home again. But I'll take if off for dinner," replied Mal.

"You have to walk ten paces behind us then," said Stacey. "Or ahead of us. But you and that headdress cannot walk *with* us."

Mal scowled. So did Jessi. "I'll walk with you," she offered, putting her arm around Mallory.

So we set out. We left the rest of my family struggling with the grill and charcoal and platters of hamburger patties and hot dogs. I walked with Mary Anne, Dawn, Stace, and Claud. Behind us were Jessi and Mallory, Mal slapping at mosquitoes with every step she took.

When we reached the lodge, we ran into the entryway and waited there while Mal stood outside and removed the netting and hat and towel and stuffed them into a shopping bag we'd made her bring along. I entertained myself by reading the bulletin board of Shadow Lake events and advertisements.

"Hey!" I cried. "You know what? We should put up a notice about the BSC."

"Here?" said Mary Anne.

"Yeah. I bet people would love to be able to hire sitters or parents' helpers. Then they could go out for a nice dinner at the lodge by themselves. Or they could go swimming or something while one of us does the housework."

"But we're on vacation," said Mary Anne.

"Oh, yeah. Right. Vacation. I forgot," I answered.

Mary Anne shook her head, but she was smiling. "Furthermore," she went on, "we're supposed to be watching eight kids of our own."

"Oh, yeah." Sometimes I get a little carried away.

When Mal was ready, my friends and I walked through the lodge to the dining room. A waiter seated us at a round table by a window. Outside, the sun was setting over the water. People were docking their boats for the night.

"Will you look at those boats?" I whispered.

"Why are you whispering?" asked Jessi.

"I don't know. Maybe some of the boats belong to the people in here." I gestured around the dining room. "And they're so fancy. The boats, I mean. They make *Faith Pierson* look sort of puny."

"I bet some of those boats are yachts," said Dawn, whispering, too.

We were unfolding our napkins and placing them in our laps, turning over our water glasses, trying to appear well-mannered and as if we were *used* to eating in restaurants by ourselves.

A waiter handed us menus. When he left, Claud said, "Did you guys see the notice about the boat show? On the bulletin board?"

We shook our heads. "Boat show?" repeated Mal.

"Yeah. You know, when people decorate their boats like floats in a parade and then they sail around the lake and everyone comes to see and some judges vote on the best float and stuff."

"There's going to be a boat show here?" I asked.

"Cool," said Dawn. "Kristy, Watson said there used to be a boat show."

"It's soon, too," Claud went on. "Saturday, I think. We should decorate *Faith Pierson* and enter her in the show."

"Enter *Faith* in the *boat* show?" I squeaked.

"Sure," said Claud.

"But the show is for yachts and other big

boats. I'm almost positive. Nobody else will be entering a little speedboat in the show. No one will even be able to see *Faith*. She'll get lost."

"I don't care. I want to decorate her anyway. It'll be fun."

"I have a better idea," I said, but just then the waiter returned.

"Ladies? Are you ready to order?" he asked.

We weren't, even though we knew the menu by heart. I looked helplessly at Stacey. She'd know how to handle the situation.

"I think we need five more minutes," Stacey told the waiter demurely.

As soon as he left, we opened our menus and scanned them. We made lightning-fast decisions — and then the waiter didn't return for fifteen minutes. After we had finally given him our order, Jessi said, "So Kristy, what's your better idea?"

"That we use *Faith* for a trip out to that island — "

"You already suggested that," Dawn interrupted me.

" — and spend the night there," I finished. "We'll camp out and return the next day. Wouldn't that be awesome?"

Dawn looked at me incredulously. She opened her mouth. She closed it. Then she opened it again. "Luckily, we cannot all fit in that speedboat at the same time," she said evenly.

"Oh, we'll figure out some way to get the BSC to the island."

"To Shadow Island," murmured Dawn. "I bet that's what it's called."

The waiter brought our food then, and a few moments later we were digging in hungrily. Except for Jessi. She was gazing across the room. I looked where she was looking . . . and my eyes came to rest on a handsome boy about Jessi's age. He was seated at a table with a younger girl, a man, and a woman — probably his sister and parents. While I was looking at him, he glanced up, turned in my direction, and smiled a smile that made his eyes sparkle. Yikes! I'd been caught staring. . . . No, the boy was smiling at Jessi, I realized, not me. And Jessi looked like she wanted to faint. Her face reddened and she ducked her head.

Hmm.

I forgot about the boy, though, when Dawn mentioned Shadow Island again. "You really want to camp out — overnight — on a haunted island?" she said to me.

"Yeah!" I looked at the rest of my friends. "Who's brave enough?" Everyone shrugged.

"Well, it would be fun," I said. "And anyway, you're the only one who thinks the island is haunted, Dawn."

Nobody seemed to want to talk much about camping out, so I dropped the subject. We talked about the boat show instead. Then, when we were leaving the lodge, we passed the bulletin board again, and Stacey exclaimed, "Hey! How'd we miss this? There's going to be a dance at the lodge!"

"While we're here?" asked Mary Anne.

"Our last night. And it says anyone can go."

Jessi's eyes widened. "Cool!" she exclaimed. "There sure is a lot to look forward to here."

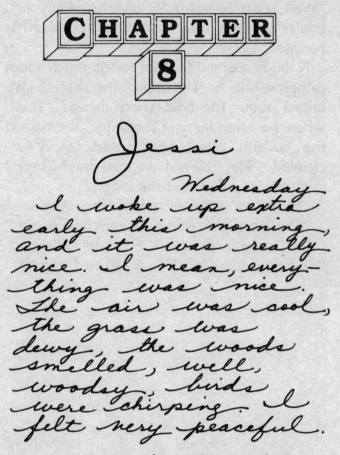

CHAPTER 8

Jessi

Wednesday

I woke up extra early this morning, and it was really nice. I mean, everything was nice. The air was cool, the grass was dewy, the woods smelled, well, woodsy, birds were chirping. I felt very peaceful.

Excuse me for interrupting your diary writing, Jessi, but let me just point out that this is the kind of entry I especially like to see. Are you paying attention, Watson? Did you

Jessi

notice that Jessi is describing
Shadow Lake as a wonderful
place? That's something to keep
in mind.

As I was saying,
the morning was
peaceful and
wonderful. I got
up before anyone
else was awake,
and I slipped
outside with my
dance things. Then
I walked along
the lake to the
lodge....

I had started practicing at the *barre* I'd found
at the lodge. Sunday morning, Monday morning, Tuesday morning, and again on Wednesday, the morning after the BSC dinner at the
lodge. The morning after the amazing evening
when *he* had noticed me, smiled at me.

Oooh, why am I thinking about these
things? I wondered as I hurried down the
road, water lapping at the shore. I have Quint.

Jessi

Remember Quint? I said to myself. You know. The boy who gave you your first real kiss? But I couldn't stop thinking of the *other* boy, picturing his face as he smiled at me, his eyes shining.

In fact, I couldn't stop thinking about him until I had begun my practice and I was stretching and bending and flexing my feet. When I felt limbered up I began a series of pliés and grands pliés. But the oddest thing happened. I kept turning my head to the right, at all the wrong times. I felt as though I were being drawn in that direction. And then I realized why. I was being watched. I wasn't alone.

I stood up after a grand plié and turned quickly to the door to the room. A figure was slouched there.

I almost screamed. Instead, I gasped. "You scared me to death."

The figure straightened up. It was the boy. He flashed his smile at me. "I'm sorry," he said. "I really didn't mean to scare you. I wanted to say something, but I didn't know whether to interrupt you."

I wasn't sure how to reply, so I didn't (and I felt like a dolt). Grow *up*, Jessi, I scolded myself.

"Do you mind if I watch you?" the boy asked.

"Well, no. I guess not." I didn't think I was doing anything terribly interesting, but if he wanted to watch, that was okay. He wouldn't make me nervous. I'm used to dancing in front of audiences. (Big ones.)

I'd brought along some tapes to use in the tape deck in the practice room. Mostly, I danced to pretty tame stuff. But I decided to cool down to rock 'n' roll. I slipped an old sixties tape into the machine and really let loose while Diana Ross and the Supremes sang about love and stuff. When the tape ended, I was surprised to hear applause. I'd forgotten about my audience.

"That was *ex*cellent!" exclaimed the boy. "Really excellent."

I shrugged. "I was just fooling around."

"Yeah? It didn't look like it." He paused. "I can't dance."

"You can't? You mean, not at all?"

"Not one step. I'm a total klutz. I wouldn't mind learning how to dance, though. Maybe I just need the right teacher. Oh — I'm Daniel," he added.

"You want a lesson?" I asked slowly. My thoughts were whirling. Was Daniel flirting with me? Well, probably, I decided. I also decided I didn't mind being flirted with by Daniel.

Then I caught myself. Where did Daniel fit into the picture? The picture of Quint and me, that is. I imagined myself with Daniel and Quint. I was standing between them, Daniel on my left, Quint on my right. I thought of the worksheets I'd been given in first grade. *What is wrong with this picture?*

"A lesson?" Daniel repeated. "Sure, I'd love a lesson."

"Right now?"

"Why not? I'm here, you're here, the music's here."

"But I don't even know you."

"And I don't even know your name."

I relaxed a little. "I'm Jessi," I said. "Jessi Ramsey. I'm here on vacation with some friends. For two weeks."

"You have an awful lot of friends," said Daniel.

I laughed. "One of my friends has a huge family. Twenty of us are here. We're staying in the big cabin near — "

"I know which one."

"You do? Do you come to Shadow Lake every summer?"

"Nope. This is the first time."

"Is that your family I've seen you with?"

Daniel nodded. "Yup. Mom, Dad, and my sister. Her name's Bridget. She's eight. And a half. Bridget is very precise."

I smiled. "I have an eight-year-old sister, too. Becca, short for Rebecca. I have a baby brother, too. We call him Squirt."

"Great name!" Daniel laughed.

"Great kid. I miss him. Becca, too."

"Where do you live?"

"Stoneybrook, Connecticut. How about you?"

"Boston."

"I've never been there. I've been to New York, though."

Daniel nodded. I cast around for another question to ask him. The only one I could come up with was, "Do people call you Dan?" Fortunately, I didn't have the chance to ask such a dumb question.

"So, how about a lesson?" said Daniel.

"Okay. Um, sure," I replied, shoving aside thoughts of Quint.

"What do I do first?"

"Take off your shoes." Mine were already off. I knew Daniel would feel freer without them.

Daniel took off his sneakers and stood awkwardly in front of me while I rewound the Diana Ross tape.

"Rule number one," I said to Daniel, grinning. "Relax. You can't dance when you're stiff. Let yourself go loose."

"Like this?"

"Well, sort of. I mean, go really *limp*. Like a wet mop."

"Oh, I get it." Daniel did loosen up.

"Rule number two," I went on. "There are no more rules."

"There aren't?" Daniel looked disappointed.

"I know you want me to tell you, 'Move your left hand like this, put your right foot over here,' and I would if I were teaching you the waltz or something, but you just want to be able to go to a school dance and have a good time, right?" Daniel nodded. "Okay, then. Listen to the music and move however you feel like moving."

"All right," said Daniel, but he hung back and watched *me* dance again.

"Come on," I said after a few moments. "Just join in."

Daniel hung back a bit longer, and then he did join in. Only he looked like a robot. "How am I doing?" he asked.

Jessi

"Um . . ." I tried to find a way to be tactful. "Pretend you have no bones in your body."

Daniel loosened up ever so slightly. "How's *this*?"

"Well, you're dancing as if a crowd of people was watching this lesson. But no one's here except me. You don't have to be self-conscious."

Ten minutes later Daniel was dancing less stiffly. It was a start.

"Whew," I said as the tape ended. "I'm exhausted. This was more of a workout than I usually give myself. Anyway, I better go. If I get back too much later my friends will probably start to worry about me."

"I'll walk you," said Daniel.

"Thanks." I gathered together my tapes and shoes and things. I was trying to sound and act extremely nonchalant. But my blood was whooshing through my veins, my heart was thudding, and my brain was thinking, "He wants to walk me home! Daniel wants to spend time with me! Daniel is flirting wi — "

Uh-oh. Daniel was *flirting* with me? I didn't need him to flirt with me. I had Quint. I would never want to hurt Quint's feelings. Besides, I really like him.

"Do you play any sports?" Daniel asked me as we were leaving the lodge.

"Sports? Nah," I replied. "Not unless you count ballet. I spend most of my spare time doing my homework, practicing, and baby-sitting. Oh, and reading. I *love* to read."

Daniel made a face. "Not me," he said. "I don't like to read unless I have to. You know, for school or something."

I nodded as if I understood, but the fact was I couldn't imagine only reading if I *had* to read. "Don't you read *any*thing except what the teachers assign?" I asked Daniel.

"Sometimes I read magazines."

"Have you ever read *The Hero and the Crown*?"

"*The Hero and the Crown*? Nope."

"How about *Maniac Magee*?"

"Never heard of it."

"Oh."

We walked in silence until Daniel said, "Do you like basketball?"

"Sometimes I watch it on TV," I replied. That was true. What I didn't add was that I thought it was a great big bore. "But I only play it when I'm taking gym. I'm afraid of twisting my ankle. Or worse, breaking my ankle. I don't know what I'd do if I couldn't dance."

"Baby-sit?" suggested Daniel, smiling.

I smiled back. "Yeah, baby-sit. I adore kids."

"So do I. . . . Well, that's not really true. I

love my sister. But I wouldn't want to change some strange kid's stinky diaper."

"The kids we sit for aren't strangers," I said. "We spend so much time with them they're like our younger brothers and sisters. Or our friends."

Daniel shrugged. "I'd still rather be playing basketball, or rollerblading down our street."

I realized then that Daniel and I had nothing in common. I also realized that I was very much enjoying hurrying through the misty Shadow Lake morning with him, watching steam rise from the water, listening to Daniel's voice, walking so close to him that the backs of our hands sometimes brushed against each other.

"Jessi? Do you want to go to the dance at the lodge?" Daniel asked me abruptly. "I mean, do you want to go with me?"

"Sure!" I answered. I didn't know whether to feel pleased or guilty.

CHAPTER 9

Mallory
⚓

I am covered with calamine lotion.

Here's what I think of when I think of the words Shadow Lake: insects. So far, I have seen mosquitoes, flies (horse flies and houseflies), chiggers, daddy longlegs, and spiders. Okay, okay. I know spiders are not insects, but I'm including them in this list since they bite just like all the other things do. That's why I'm covered with calamine — because under the calamine I'm covered with bites, most of which itch, all of which look disgusting.

Excuse me, Mal, for taking the diary out of your hands, but don't you have anything nice to say about Shadow Lake? After all, Watson will be reading this and ... you know.

I know, Kristy. It's just that

The good stuff, Mal. The good stuff

Well, the lake is beautiful.

That's more like it.

83

Let me finish! The lake is beautiful. The woods are beautiful. The weather is beautiful. Now if only David Michael and Linny and my brother could stop arguing for three minutes.

You are hopeless, Mallory.

I was hopeless? Was it my fault so many bugs had taken up residence at Shadow Lake? Was it my fault they bit me more than they bit everyone else combined? Actually, that *was* sort of strange. Why did the bugs choose me? Did I do something to attract them? Was I somehow advertising myself as the Mallory Pike Bug Restaurant? Or the Mallory Pike Blood Bank?

I had been *so* excited about this vacation, but since I'd arrived, I'd spent most of my time experimenting with insect repellent and devising other ways to keep bugs off me. I thought the safari hat over the towel was ingenious, but everyone else thought I looked dorky. Even Jessi, although she didn't come right out and say so. She's much too polite to do something like that.

Wednesday of our first week at the lake was my day to keep an eye on Nicky, Linny, and David Michael. Of course they wanted to play outdoors. I'd expected that, yet some microscopic part of my brain had hoped they'd say, "Mallory? We want to stay inside today, okay? We are going to write letters and read and play Parcheesi."

Fat chance. The sky was a clear blue, and by the time we'd finished breakfast, the thermometer already read 79°. What kid would want to miss that weather? Not David Michael, Linny, or my brother.

"You guys," I said to the boys as everyone else scattered from the cabin to begin another busy day, "you'll have to wait a minute. I need to put on some extra clothes before we go out."

"Oh, no," said my brother, groaning. "You're not putting on that beekeeper outfit, are you?" He grimaced.

"Yes, I am putting on that beekeeper outfit," I replied testily. "You know I have to. Unless you want me to blow up like a balloon from all the bites I'll get. And all the stings."

Nicky pretended to think this over. "Let's see," he said. "Beekeeper or balloon. Which do I want my sister to look like?"

"Nicky — " I began.

"Oh, I guess I'll take the beekeeper. We'll wait outside for you." *We* meant the three boys. They refused to play with girls or with anyone younger than they were, which eliminated everyone except Sam and Charlie who were interested *only* in girls. (Well, and in waterskiing.)

I ran into the girls' bedroom. I was already wearing jeans, a long-sleeved shirt, socks, and sneakers. Now I added the hat, the towel, the mosquito netting, and gardening gloves, after a good dose of bug spray. To be on the safe side, I tied a large kerchief around my neck. I wished for a way to protect my face better, but couldn't think of anything. Besides, the boys were growing impatient. I could hear them arguing on the porch.

"Settle down!" I yelled to them. "I'll be right there."

The boys spent most of the morning swimming in the lake and diving off the dock, despite the fact that the water really *was* freezing, as far as I was concerned. (Kristy's stepfather said it probably wouldn't feel warm until August.) *I* spent the morning trying to find the least bug-ridden spot from which to supervise the boys. I went back and forth between a lawn chair on the shore, and a towel spread on the end of the dock. In the chair I was bothered by gnats and flies. On the dock I was bothered by mosquitos.

I couldn't win.

Plus, no one (and I mean *no* one) would come near me.

"You smell," said my brother.

"You're an embarrassment," added Kristy.

Jessi was somewhat more sympathetic. "*I'd* sit near you," she said, "but I'm in charge of Emily and Andrew today, and I promised them a walk to the lodge to buy some candy."

I tried not to mind. Anyway, the boys kept me busy breaking up their many arguments. They were trying to impress and outdo one another.

"I can hold my breath underwater longer than you guys can!" Linny would shout. Then he'd call out, "Time me!" and duck beneath the surface of the lake. When he'd come up for air, he'd say, "How long was that?" and look expectantly at David Michael who was wearing a waterproof stopwatch on one wrist.

"Twelve seconds!" David Michael would reply.

"No way! That was twenty seconds easy!"

"Was not!"

"Was too!"

"Who cares?" spoke up Nicky. "I can hold my breath for twenty-*five* seconds. Time me, you guys!" Then Nicky would duck underwater, David Michael would time him, and (when he heard the results) my brother would accuse David Michael of not being able to read his own watch. "Cheater!" he would add.

"Listen, you guys," I said to the boys after their fifth or sixth argument, "can't you just *play?* Why does everything have to be a contest? You aren't here to challenge each other. You're here to have fun."

For a full four minutes, the boys didn't argue. (They didn't talk, either, but I was glad for the peace and quiet.) Then Nicky cannonballed off the dock, landing inches from where Linny was on his back, practicing floating. The cannonball not only splashed Linny, it startled him out of his floating position.

"Cut it out, jerk!" Linny shouted at Nicky.

"Cut what out?" Nicky climbed onto the dock again and cannonballed back into the lake. "You mean that?" he asked. "Is that what you want me to cut out?"

"Yes!"

"Just checking," said my brother.

"Nicky," I said warningly.

"Yeah, *Nicky*," mimicked Linny.

I sighed. Why couldn't the boys get along? I had hoped the trip to the lake would be good for my brother. Sometimes he has trouble fitting in with our family. At home he also won't play with the "girls" (our sisters), and the triplets usually don't want to play with Nicky because he's younger. So he's often on his own. But on this vacation he had built-in friends. Only the boys spent more time fighting than playing.

Maybe they needed to try a different activity. What could I suggest that would be different and fun?

"Hey, guys?" I called. "How would you like to go fishing?"

"Fishing? Really?" replied Linny.

"Sure," cried David Michael and Nicky.

We returned to the cabin for fishing gear, then headed for a spot on the lake that Mitch assured us would guarantee bites. For twenty minutes or so, the boys were busy getting settled, baiting their hooks, and peering into the lake, trying to *see* where the fish were. Twenty minutes after that, David Michael caught the first fish.

"All *right!*" I cheered from my spot on the shore. (I wasn't fishing. I was too involved with my calamine lotion, bug spray, safari hat, and mosquito netting.)

David Michael was still untangling his prize from the hook when Nicky caught a fish. I cheered for him, too. "All *right!*" But Linny scowled at him over his shoulder. "Show-off," he muttered.

And that was the beginning of yet another argument. Four arguments later I had had enough — of both the boys *and* the bugs. "Attention!" I shouted. "Nicky! Linny! David Michael! Time to pack up your gear. We're going back to the cabin!"

"Already?" whined my brother.

"Yes, and don't whine," I said.

"Baby," added Linny.

I led the trio of dejected boys away from Shadow Lake and back to their dorm in the cabin. "I want you to stay here for fifteen minutes," I told them. "Try to be civil with each other. You're supposed to be friends."

"I'm — " Linny began, but I cut him off.

I headed for the girls' bedroom, intending to collapse on my bed and enjoy a few moments of peace. Hopefully, bug-free peace.

No such luck. The room was not empty. Claud, Stacey, and Jessi were in it. They were reading magazines and giggling.

"Nice outfit," Claud said as I entered the room. "I like the gardening gloves. They're a lovely touch."

"Oh, shut up."

"Ooh, testy." (That was Stacey.)

"You shut up, too!" I exclaimed.

"Mal!" cried Jessi. "What is the matter?"

"What's the matter? Everyone is fighting

and I look like the poster child for Bug-Off spray. That's what's the matter."

Jessi pulled me out of the room. "You and I are taking a walk," she announced.

As Jessi and I ambled along the edge of the lake, I told her about the boys.

"Well, just because *they're* cranky doesn't mean *you* have to be cranky," she pointed out. "And your bug bites *are* going to go away," she added before I could say anything further about them.

"I know, I know. . . . Jessi? Do you mind if we go back now? I'm getting bitten again. Maybe by dragonflies. Do they bite? Or maybe by chiggers or mosquitos or . . ."

CHAPTER 10

DAVID MICHAEL

THURSDAY

TODAY WE FOUND A FORT. ONLY
WE CANNOT USE IT. THAT IS NOT
FAIR. ALSO IT IS NOT FUN. SOMETHING
ELSE THAT IS NOT FUN IS MY FRIENDS
LINNY AND NICKY. THEY WILL NOT
STOP FIGTHING. THEY FIGTH WHILE
WE SWIM AND WHEN WE WENT
FISHING. I THOUGT WE COULD WORK
ON THE FORT TOGETHER AND THEY
WOULD STOP FIGTHING ONLY NOW
WE CAN'T WORK ON THE FORT
EITHER BUT WE ARE GOING TO BILD
OUR OWN FORTE SO MAYBE THEY
WILL STOP FIGTHING SOON.

Linny and Nicky just argued and fought almost all the time. I did not understand this. Linny is one of my best friends. So is Nicky. If they are both my good friends, why did they fight so much? Maybe because they didn't know each other very well. They knew *me*, but not each *other*. I decided we needed a project. We needed something we could do together, something all of us liked doing. Also, something we couldn't argue about. Something that wouldn't make us say, "I can do that better than you!" Or, "I can do that faster than you!"

I thought for awhile. I got an idea.

"Let's take Shannon on a walk," I said to Linny and Nicky.

It was Thursday. We had been at the lake for five whole days. We let Shannon outside several times each day, but someone always went with her. Since she did not know her way around Shadow Lake we were afraid she would get lost. I decided she might want a nice long walk in the woods, though. Shannon had not spent much time in real woods.

"On a walk?" repeated Nicky. "A walk to where?"

"Who cares?" said Linny.

"Shannon might care."

93

"Yeah, right."

"A walk in the woods, you guys," I said. "And cut it out!"

"Shannon would like the woods," said Nicky thoughtfully.

"I'll ask Kristy if we can go without her," I said. "I mean, without Kristy." I did not understand why my sister had to baby-sit us. Or why any of her friends had to baby-sit us. We don't need sitters. Karen does, Andrew does, Emily Michelle does. But not *us*. I hoped Kristy would let us take just one single walk without her.

"We'll stay near the cabin," I said to her. "We won't go too far."

"But I'm in charge of you."

"Can't you be in charge of us from the cabin? You could even sit out on the back porch. Then you would hear us if we yelled for help from the woods. We'd yell 'S-O-S!' and you could come after us. Anyway, we're taking Shannon on a walk, so we'll have her for protection."

"Shannon is not a watch dog," said my sister. "She adores everyone, even strangers. If she saw any kind of danger she'd probably run up to it and cover it with puppy kisses."

"Okay. Then we'd yell S-O-S, like I said."

"Let me check with Mom or Watson." Kristy

ran out the front door and down to the lake where Mom was swimming near the dock. They yelled back and forth to each other. Then Kristy returned to the cabin. "Mom said you guys can go by yourselves — "

"Yes!" I cried.

" — if I really do sit out on the porch and if you promise not to go very far and if you also promise to come back in half an hour."

"I promise. I mean, we promise!"

"All right. I'll be timing you."

"Let's symbolize our watches."

"Synchronize," Kristy corrected me. "That's a good idea."

So we set our watches. Then I snapped Shannon's leash to her collar. Linny, Nicky, Shannon, and I stood at the edge of the yard.

"Go!" yelled my sister.

We disappeared into the woods. I unclipped Shannon's leash so she could run free. "Have fun!" I yelled as she scampered off.

I think Shannon really did have fun. Nicky and Linny and I could hear her sniffing and whuffling around. Soon I could hear another kind of sound, too. Voices? Maybe. I hoped I would not have to shout S-O-S. I hoped Shannon would turn out to be a watch dog.

I elbowed Linny and Nicky. "Shhh!" I hissed.

"What?" asked Nicky.

"Just be quiet for a sec. Listen."

Linny and Nicky and I stood very still. We listened hard.

Linny's eyes grew wide. "Voices!" he whispered.

"They're coming from over there." Nicky pointed through the trees.

We crept toward the voices. Soon we could see a . . . fort! "Cool!" I said under my breath. "Excellent!"

"Yeah, but someone's in it," Linny reminded me.

While we stood looking at the wooden shack someone ran out of it.

It was Karen, my sister.

"What's *she* doing there?" whispered Linny.

I shrugged my shoulders. "Don't know. But let's find out. . . . Oh, and sneak up on her. We can scare her while we're at it."

Karen had sat down on the ground near the shack. She looked like she might be weeding. But who weeds woods?

Shannon came bounding back to us, so I picked her up (even though Shannon is absolutely enormous for a puppy) and Nicky and Linny and I tiptoed up behind Karen. When we were just a couple of feet away I looked at my friends. I nodded. Then the three of us screamed, "Boo!"

Karen *was* weeding. And when we shouted, she jumped and threw a handful of dirty roots and leaves in the air.

"Aughh!" shrieked Karen.

"What's the matter?" called another voice.

"Yeah, what happened?"

Hannie and Nancy ran out of the fort.

"Hey, what are you guys doing?" demanded Hannie. (She was mostly looking at Linny, her brother.)

"What are *you* guys doing?" Linny asked the girls.

"Working on our playhouse. And fixing up our garden," Karen replied. "They used to be a *secret* playground and a *secret* garden, but I guess they aren't anymore." She scowled.

"Playhouse!" I repeated. "That isn't any playhouse. It's a fort."

"Yeah," agreed Linny and Nicky.

The girls shook their heads. "No way. It's a playhouse."

"And it's ours," added Nancy.

"Who says?" I wanted to know.

"Finders keepers. We got here first."

"But you're just using it for a dumb playhouse," I went on. "We could make it into a cool fort — for boys only."

"It's already for *girls* only," said Karen. "Why should we give it up? Why should we let you have it? Huh?"

"Well, why should *you* have it? It doesn't really belong to you. You just found it here in the woods. And," I went on, before Nancy could say, "Finders keepers," again, "you probably don't know anything about it. Maybe it belongs to someone *else*. Maybe you are . . . trespassing."

Karen paused. Then she said, "Oh, we are *not*. You can't scare me."

"I just did. Remember? Boo?"

"Well, anyway, Daddy and Elizabeth said we could play in the shack."

"If we'd asked first, they would have said the boys could have the shack."

"But you did not ask," said Hannie.

"We didn't *know* about the shack," retorted Linny.

"Look, how about if we *share* the shack?" I suggested.

"No! You boys will turn it into a fort!"

"Will not!"

"So you'll help us decorate it like a tiny, pretty cottage in the woods?"

"We-ell . . . We want to build stuff, not decorate."

"If you guys want to build so much, then go build your own fort. I dare you," said Karen. She put her hands on her hips and glared at me.

"Okay, we will," I said.

"Yeah," said Nicky and Linny. (Finally they had agreed on something.)

"And you know what else? Our fort will be better than your playhouse, better than this old shack."

"How much?" said Hannie.

"How much better?" asked her brother.

"No! How much do you want to *bet* that your fort will be better than our playhouse? The Three Musketeers are betting you."

"Wait — I don't have any money," said Nicky. "Well, not much."

"Me neither," I said. "Okay, gentleman's bet."

"No way!" cried Karen. "A gentleman's bet is no fun. How about . . . if we win, the girls get to sleep in *both* the big bedrooms, so we can each have a whole bunk of our own. You boys will have to sleep on the couches in the living room."

"Okay," I said. "And if the *boys* win, you

girls will have to do all our chores for a month."

"A month!" exclaimed Nancy. "Wait a sec. Then us girls change our part of the bet. If we win, you have to do *our* chores for a month."

"We'll do them for the rest of the summer," I said boldly.

"We will?" said Nicky.

"You will?" said Hannie. "How come?"

"Because the boys are going to win. This is a sure bet."

"Shake on it," commanded Nancy.

Nicky and Linny and I shook hands with Hannie, Nancy, and Karen. "Now the bet is legal," I announced.

"Where are you going to build your fort?" asked Karen.

"Somewhere in the woods. That's all we will tell you. We want to build it in privacy. No girls allowed."

"Well, no *help* allowed for *you*," said Karen. "You can't ask Watson or Kristy or Mitch or anyone to help you."

"We don't need help," Linny replied haughtily.

I looked at my watch then. "Hey, we have to take Shannon back to the cabin. Our time is almost up." I cupped my hands around my mouth. "Shannon! Shannon! Here, girl!" I heard a yip. Then Shannon bounded out of the underbrush. I fastened her leash onto her collar again.

" 'Bye!" called Karen. "Good riddance!"

Linny and Nicky and Shannon and I started to walk away, but I turned around long enough to shout, "So long, suckers!" Then I ran back to the cabin with my friends. (We got there just in time.) I could not wait for us to begin our project together.

Claudia

Thrusday

Emily, michele and Andrew and I took a walk to the boat dock today. Guess waht people are geting there boots ready for the big boat shoe on satruday. So I started thicking abust how to fix up faith Person for the show. Andrea had ideas too he had lot of them. Emily did not have ideos but she had fun. Emil and Andrew are good kids. Kirsty is very lucky. Oh and may I add that Shadew Lack is a very wonderful wonderfull place, Watson.

I wasn't kidding about Shadow Lake. I really do think it's a wonderful place. It's beautiful, the air smells good, there's lots to do, the cabin is nice and so is the lodge, and *Faith Pierson* is really fun. Mitch taught Kristy how to drive the boat. Now he's teaching Sam, and next he might teach me.

Thursday was my day to be in charge of Emily and Andrew. I had thought they would want to go swimming (well, wading), but Andrew said no. "Let's do something different today."

"Okay," I replied. "What do you guys feel like doing?" We had just finished breakfast and were sitting on a big swing on the porch.

Emily Michelle looked at me and grinned. "Fim?" she suggested.

"No, Andrew is tired of fimming. I mean, swimming."

"Can we go see the boats?" Andrew asked.

"The boats?"

"You know, the parked ones."

"Oh, the boats at the boat dock," I said. "Sure. We can walk to the dock. That's a good idea. Emily, do you want to look at some boats?"

"Boats!" she cried. (That must have meant yes.)

I decided to bring my sketch pad with me. Who knew what I might see.

"Are you going to draw?" asked Andrew as he watched me put the pad and some pencils and charcoals into a tote bag.

"Yup."

"Can I draw, too?"

Not a bad idea. "Okay," I agreed. "I'll put some of your paper and crayons and markers in here with my stuff. Then you and Emily can draw boats and the lake and anything else you feel like. We can pretend we're artists."

"Yes!" exclaimed Andrew. "Do you have easels for us?"

I shook my head. "Sorry, no easels. No berets for our heads, either. We can pretend we are *starving* artists."

Andrew frowned. "I don't get it."

I tried to explain "starving artists" to him while he and Emily and I walked along the shore of Shadow Lake in the direction of the dock. I guess I wasn't doing a good job (or maybe I was just being boring) because Andrew interrupted me in the middle of ". . . so artists do not usually work for companies. They are freelancers. That means — "

"Hey, Claudia, look!" Andrew cried.

"Yook!" Emily added.

"What?" I asked.

"Over there! A turtle is on that rock. He's just sitting there."

"I think he likes the sunshine," I said.

"Is he getting a tan?"

"Well, probably not. He's snoozing."

The turtle made me think of other animals I had seen at the lake which made me think of Noah's Ark which made me think of boats which made me think of the boat show. Noah's Ark would be a good theme for decorating a boat. In fact, it might be a good theme for *Faith Pierson* — or not. Not, I decided. Where was I going to get thousands of pairs of animals? Okay, if Noah's Ark wouldn't work, what *could* work? As Andrew and Emily and I sauntered along, I thought about other "costumes" for *Faith Pierson*. How else could I dress her up?

"Claudia?" said Andrew. "You are frowning. What are you thinking about?"

"Oh, I didn't mean to frown. Sorry, Andrew. I was thinking about the boat show, the one on Saturday. Kristy explained it to you, remember? The boats will be in a parade on the lake."

"Oh, yeah."

"And I am going to put *Faith Pierson* in the show."

"Our boat? You are?"

"Yup. Kristy is going to drive her. But first I have to figure out how to decorate her. I have to do something extra good."

"Decorate her for Christmas!" exclaimed Andrew.

"Well, I — "

"No, for Thanksgiving. Wait — make *Faith Pierson* look like a turkey!"

"Andrew!" I giggled.

"Or you could decorate her like a pirate," Andrew went on. "That's what I want to be for Halloween."

A pirate. Hmm. Maybe a pirate *ship?* That would be fun, but hard to do. I'd need an awful lot of people to play pirates, and the boat does not hold many people.

"Keep thinking," I told Andrew.

"Okay," he answered. And he did think. By the time we reached the boat dock he had suggested decorating *Faith Pierson* as a crayon, a hobo, Gumby, and a Hershey bar.

I liked that last idea, but knew it would not work, and neither would the others. Meanwhile, I didn't come up with any good ideas of my own. A lot of other people had good ideas, though. How did I know? Because about half of the boats at the dock were being decorated for the show. *Really* decorated.

"Wow!" cried Andrew. "That boat is going

to be New York City, I think." (He was pointing.) "And that one looks like a western movie. I see a cactus and a cowboy hat and cowboy boots and one of those rope things."

"A lasso," I murmured, not really paying attention. I knew I should start working on *Faith Pierson* right away. Maybe I would get an idea if I sketched for awhile. That sometimes helps.

I sat on a wooden bench and pulled my paper out of the tote bag. "Emily? Andrew?" I said. "I'm going to draw."

"Good," replied Andrew. "Then so are we."

Excellent. I had just realized I couldn't let them go wandering around by themselves. They weren't wearing life preservers.

The three of us sat in a row. Idly, I sketched whatever I saw while Andrew drew a red sailboat floating on a blue sea, and Emily drew a design of scribbles using every single marker in the box.

"Lovely," I said to her. "Can you tell me about your picture?" (That's a safe question when you don't know what a kid's picture is *of*, and you don't want to hurt any feelings.)

"Teddy bear," said Emily clearly. (Good imagination.)

The three of us returned to our drawings.

Emily finished her scribbles and painstakingly wrote the letter E in the lower left corner of the paper. I am teaching her to write her name. (The E is a good beginning.) Sometimes I tutor Emily Michelle to help her catch up with other kids her age. I might seem like a funny choice for a tutor since I can barely spell, but the thing is, I was the one who taught Emily how to match, to name colors, and of course to write that E. Emily is proud of her accomplishments. And I'm proud to be able to help her with her accomplishments. Now if I could just get a good idea for the boat show.

I glanced up from my sketches in time to see Emily hand her drawing to Andrew. "You," she said.

"For me?" Andrew replied.

Emily nodded. "Thank you."

"No, *I* say thank you," Andrew told her.

"I say thank you," Emily repeated obediently.

"No!" Andrew looked frustrated. Then he said pointedly, *"Thank you."*

"Thank you," said Emily. She smiled.

"You say you're welcome."

"You say you're welcome."

"No, I say thank you."

"I say thank you."

"Claudia!" complained Andrew.

"Let's move on to a different subject," I suggested.

"Okay. I know. The boat show. Maybe you could decorate *Faith Pierson* like, um, like — " (Andrew looked across the lake) " — like the lake."

"Well . . . we're already *at* the lake," I pointed out. "These other boat themes don't have anything to do with the lake. Hmm. Maybe I could just put flowers all over the boat. I could call it the Flower Garden."

"Maybe," said Andrew.

"Or maybe a beach theme. I could make a palm tree, and Kristy and I could wear jams and our new extra-dark shades."

"Do something more fun," said Andrew. (That's one reason I like kids. They're so honest.) "Do something big. I like that New York boat. And the cowboy boat. *You* do a cowboy boat."

"I don't want to copy," I replied. "Besides, I don't think I can decorate *Faith Pierson* with a theme like New York or the Wild West. *Faith Pierson* is too small."

Emily capped the marker she'd been using to scribble her second picture. She tossed it back into its box. Then she jumped to her feet. "Go?" she said. "Go?"

"Do you want to look at the boats again?"
I asked her.

Emily shook her head. "Home."

"Emily. Stoneybrook is *miles* away," said
Andrew witheringly.

"I think she just wants to go back to our
cabin," I told him. "Are you ready to go, too?"

"Okay," replied Andrew.

So we packed up our gear and walked along
the dock. This is another thing about kids (little ones, that is). Their attention spans are not
very long.

On our way to the cabin we ran into Stacey
and Dawn. They were wearing their bathing
suits and walking in the direction of the dock,
towels rolled up under their arms. Stacey was
frowning furiously.

"Hey, you guys," I greeted them. "Where
are you going?"

"Away from Sam," Stacey snapped. "As far
as possible."

"Sam is bugging her," added Dawn. "He
will not leave her alone. Poor thing, she can't
even swim by our own dock."

"Oh. Well, wherever you're going, see if
you can think of a theme for the boat show."

"Okay. And you keep your eyes peeled for
the Lake Monster," replied Dawn.

Lunacy! I was living with lunacy!

CHAPTER 12

Sam

Friday

Shadow Lake is awesome and I am not just saying that. I mean it. Charlie and I have not been bored for a second. There is so much to do here. The best things are water sports, I have even been para-sailing now, which was way cool. I wish I could write more about the best feature of the lake scene, but I cant. Sorry. It's private. Although, in my family, nothing is private for long. Actually, everyone probably knows my secret by now.

(I am writing this a long time after Sam finished his entry in the diary. What is he, crazy? Of course we know what he thinks is the best feature of the lake. He has not been subtle *about it. On the other hand, I, Kristy Thomas, happen to be fairly astute. I have not been a little sister all my life for nothing.)*

Friday was a typical day for Charlie and me. I mean, a typical day at Shadow Lake, which is not typical of too much else. We slept as late as possible, for starters. At home, alone in my room, I could have slept until nine-thirty easily. But here in the boys' dorm, I woke up just a little after seven.

Someone was singing.

And someone was singing a really stupid song. It went like this: "Woop, woop, woop. Gummity, gummity, woop, woop. Woop-de-doop-de-doop-de-doop. Gummity, gummity, woop."

For a moment, I thought Karen had somehow wound up in the wrong bedroom. That song was just the kind that little sister of mine would invent. And then sing until she drove everybody up the wall. Maybe she'd gotten up to use the bathroom during the night and had found her way into the boys' . . . No. Not very likely.

I heaved myself onto one elbow and peered around from my place on a top bunk. All I could see was us boys. The singer was Andrew.

Oh, no! It was a hereditary problem. Andrew was going to wind up just like Karen. I wasn't sure I could take *two* of them.

"Andrew!" I hissed. "Shh! It's not even seven-thirty. This is vacation. People are trying to sleep."

"Not me."

"Not *I*," I corrected him. "But you aren't the only one here."

"Too late," mumbled Charlie from the next bunk over.

"*Much* too late," added David Michael.

Since we were awake, we decided to get up and get going. Charlie and I waited until the little kids had used the bathroom. Then we went in together. While I brushed my teeth, Charlie shaved.

I don't need to shave yet, but the day is coming. I can feel it. And I'll be prepared when it arrives. I've been paying close attention to shaving-cream commercials. I think they're fascinating, which should tell you something. I mean, ordinarily, who could care less about *any* commercial? But when I turned fifteen, car commercials suddenly became mesmerizing, and then *bam!* Three weeks later, so did shaving-cream commercials. Also commercials for razors. I have been doing some research on shaving stuff — like, what does the best job and is the least expensive? What smells the best? What do most of the senior boys at SHS wear? Does anyone my age use after-shave?

Now I've bought a razor and some cream, and instead of after-shave, a miniscule bottle of men's cologne. I'm just waiting for whiskers.

Charlie's got whiskers. (Sort of.) *He's* been shaving for a few months now. I watch him as often as possible so as to be able to use his shaving style from the start.

"Want to go para-sailing today?" I asked Charlie, as I screwed the top back on the toothpaste and hung my brush in the holder.

"Hmm." Charlie considered the suggestion. "How about waterskiing? We only tried that once so far."

"Okay. Great." Charlie and I have lived in or on the lake pretty much since we arrived here last weekend.

Charlie patted his face dry. Then he left the bathroom. I followed him to the door, checked to make sure no one was around, then closed the door. I crept to the sink and examined my face in the mirror. Not one whisker yet. Not *one*. How long am I going to have to wait? I wondered.

Oh, well. Even if I didn't need to shave, there was nothing wrong with *smelling* like I needed to shave. Carefully, I applied a little of that cologne to my face. Then I sniffed my hands. Ah. Manly.

Maybe *now* Stacey would pay attention to me.

Breakfast that morning was as noisy as ever. And we were even eating outside on the porch where the trees could absorb some of the sound. Think how noisy we would have sounded if we'd been *in*doors. Mostly, we were talking about our plans for the day.

"The Three Musketeers are going to play in our wonderful playhouse," said Karen. "And tend the garden," she added, sounding as if she were repeating something she'd read in a book.

"Well, us boys are going to work on our fort," said David Michael, "which is going to be a much funner place to play."

"I have to think of what to do with *Faith Pierson* today," spoke up Claudia.

"Who's Faith Pierson?" asked Charlie.

"Our boat, dummy," answered Kristy.

"Oh, yeah."

Charlie and I had been so wrapped up in our water sports that we had barely paid attention to anything else. Now Charlie said to Kristy and her friends, "You mean you guys are entering *that* little thing — " (he meant *Faith Pierson*) " — in the parade with all those yachts and houseboats?"

"*Yes,*" Claudia answered defensively. "So what?"

"Nothing," muttered Charlie.

I glanced discreetly across the table at Stacey to see what her reaction to the discussion was. When I couldn't tell, I snapped my spoon back and fired a wet Cheerio at her. It landed on her toast.

"Gross, Sam!" she cried. "Would you cut that out? What a pest!"

I am not sure I'm a pest, but I do admit I make pretty good goof calls. My favorite one is to keep calling somebody's number and saying, "Hi, is Joe there?" (You can use any name.) Then, when whoever has been answering your calls is good and annoyed, you phone one last time and say, "Hi, this is Joe. Have there been any calls for me?" Another one I like, and this is really simple (and not actually a goof call, which should sit well with parents), is just to answer the phone by saying, "Thomas summer home. Some are home, some are not."

Okay, so maybe I do have a reputation as a . . . well, I'm not sure as a what. But why can't Stacey treat me like something more than a pesky fly? I wouldn't have been surprised if she'd gotten dressed in Mallory's bug outfit and chased me with a flyswatter.

Did I remember to mention that I like Stacey? I don't mean I just like her, the way I like most people. I mean I *like* like her. Even if I am in high school and she's still in middle school. I can't help it. What's not to *like* like about Stacey? First of all, she seems older than she is. Hard to believe she and Kristy are the same age. Second, Stacey is gorgeous, but that isn't why I like her. I know plenty of gorgeous girls I don't *like* like — because of what's inside. Stacey's beautiful smile and great hair are just icing on the cake. (Her clothes are decorations on the icing, I guess.) No, there's something about Stacey's spirit or whatever. It appeals to me, even when she's calling me a pest or rolling her eyes or actually running away from me, like she did yesterday. When that happened, by the way, I decided that if I accomplished only one thing on this vacation, it would be to let Stacey know how I feel about her. I'd been trying, but I guess I hadn't gotten the point across to her.

I said so to Charlie later that morning after we'd been waterskiing.

"Sam," said Charlie, "I've been watching you this week. I know what's going on. Have you actually *told* Stacey how you feel about her? Or have you just whistled at her and shot Cheerios onto her toast?"

"Well . . . mostly it's been, you know, the Cheerios and stuff."

"Then *talk* to her."

"Okay." I paused. "You mean talking to her is the next step? I was going to try accidentally running into her and knocking her down. If that didn't work, I was going to sort of push her into the lake and then dive in and save her."

"Believe me, she wouldn't appreciate either one. Besides, she can swim. If you toss her in the lake you'll just ruin her watch or something, and then she'll be mad at you. Again."

"Oh, yeah."

I spent the rest of the day swimming, tanning, and eating. I did not find a single opportunity to talk to Stacey alone (which shouldn't surprise you). When dinner was over and everyone had returned from the lodge and was beginning to flake out, I decided to take a walk. I thought maybe I should prepare a speech for whenever I did get to talk to Stacey.

So I crossed the path to the dock — and there she was. Her back was facing me. She was sitting at the end of the dock, swinging her feet in the water and watching the clouds turn from pink to gold to gray as the sun set.

"Stacey?" I said.

She didn't even turn around. She just buried her face in her hands and moaned, "Oh, no." But after a few moments she did look at me. "What? You're not going to whistle at me? Or tell me I look impeccable or something?"

"Nope." I walked along the dock until I was standing behind Stacey.

"Well, what are you waiting for?" she said. "Go ahead. Push me in."

"And I wasn't going to push you in the water, either."

"Okay. I know. You're making a sort of person-to-person goof call."

"No! Look, I understand why you'd expect something like that, but . . . Stacey, do you mind if I sit next to you?"

She sighed. "No. Not if that's all you're going to do."

"I just want to talk to you," I told her as I sat down. I swung my feet in the water, too. "The sky's really pretty, isn't it?"

"Yeah. You know something? Whenever I see a gorgeous sunset like this, I wonder how I could ever have felt I never wanted to leave New York. But when I'm in the city, in the middle of the action and excitement, I wonder how I could ever have moved to Connecticut."

I smiled. "I know what you mean. At least, I think I do."

"So what did you want to talk about?" Stacey still looked suspicious.

"Well, actually I wanted to talk about us." (Stacey raised her eyebrows.) "I guess I might as well just say it. I like you, Stacey." Before she could plunge in and say, "I like you, too, Sam," I went on, "I mean, I don't just like you. I *like* like you." I glanced at her.

At first I couldn't see any reaction. She continued to gaze across the water. Then after a few moments, she turned to me slowly. "You have a funny way of showing it. You tease me, you embarrass me — "

"I know, I know. I'm sorry," I broke in.

"Sam, you know what? You play so many jokes on people that I don't know whether to believe you even now. For all I know, this is just another big joke. David Michael's proba-

121

bly hiding somewhere nearby recording our conversation on a tape player."

"He is not!" I exclaimed, sounding more like someone Andrew's age than a high school student.

"You know, I liked you once," said Stacey. "I did. I'm not sure if you remember the time. It was more than a year ago, when I was in seventh grade and I'd just moved here from New York. I had a crush on you, Sam. And I don't care who knows," she added, glancing around. (For spies and hidden tape recorders, I guess.)

"Really? How do you feel about me now?"

Stacey frowned. "Confused," she said finally.

"Oh." Me too. We must have been on different timetables.

CHAPTER 13

Mary Anne

Friday

Today I watched The
Three Musketeers again.
And if I do say so
myself, I came up with
a brilliant baby-sitting
activity. I told the
girls they were going to
be my sitters. They loved
the idea. For once,
they had a chance to
boss around a big person.
So they took me swimming,
took me for a walk in
the woods, and also took
every opportunity to tell
me how to behave!

Mary Anne

When breakfast was over on Friday morning, I expected Karen, Nancy, and Hannie to run out of the cabin, yelling, "We're going to work on our playhouse!" as they had done the past few mornings. Instead, they wandered onto the front porch, Karen flopped onto a lounge chair, and Hannie and Nancy climbed into the wicker swing.

"What's up, you guys?" I asked. I was standing in the entryway to the porch. A copy of *The Wind in the Willows* was in my hand, one finger marking my place. (I'd read the book before, and I'm sure I'll read it again.) I was preparing to read on the back porch while the girls played in the woods — without a sitter, as they had been requesting. But apparently today would be different.

"We are a teensy bit bored," said Karen.

"Yeah, we're tired of our secret house," said Nancy.

"And our secret garden," added Hannie.

"You are?" I asked.

"I guess just for today," said Karen. "We want to do other stuff."

"We have not been swimming very much," pointed out Hannie, who loves to swim. She says she wants to be an Olympic swimmer one day. "We have hardly been to the lake at all."

"Well, let's take care of that," I said. And (for whatever reason) that was when my brainstorm came along. "I have an idea!" I exclaimed. "Today, how about if you three be the baby-sitters, and I'll be little Mary Anne, and *you* can take care of *me*?"

"You mean boss you around?" said Hannie, her eyes gleaming.

"Sort of," I said. "You will be in charge of me."

"All *right!*" cried Nancy. "I always wanted to be in charge of someone. At home, someone is always in charge of me. . . . I am an only child, you know. I don't have a little brother or sister to boss around."

"I do," said Karen, "but that is not as much fun as being a sitter."

"Yeah," agreed Hannie. "Okay. When do we start?"

"Right now," I answered. "And you guys are my sitters until nine tonight. Or until you get tired of being my sitters."

The girls stared at me. Hannie said, "Wait. We can't be your sitters yet. You are too big. You should crawl around like a baby."

"That's a good idea," I said, "but I don't think I can crawl all day."

"Babies do," Nancy pointed out.

"I know, but I'm thirteen. My knees are

125

weak. Can't I just be a very tall baby who can already walk and talk — a little? You can still be my sitters. And boss me around."

"Okay," agreed Hannie.

"What are we going to do today?" I asked in a high, little-girl voice.

"We are going to do very many activities," replied Karen, speaking for the group, and sounding like a grown woman. "First we are going to . . . um, I better check with my — with my helpers." The Three Musketeers huddled in a corner for a moment. Then they turned to me, and Karen announced, "First we are going to take a hike in the woods."

"Okay, I'm ready!" I cried. "Yea! A hike!" I started to leave the porch.

A hand reached out and grabbed my wrist. "Just a second!" said Nancy. "Young lady, you are not going hiking in bare feet. Go back in the cabin and put on shoes and socks. I don't want any lymey old ticks to get on you. And wear a sun hat!"

"And bring a sweat shirt," said Hannie. "The woods might be cool."

"And be sure to go to the bathroom," added Nancy. "There are no bathrooms in the woods, no matter how hard you look."

"But *we* do not have to bring sweat shirts or go to the bathroom first," said Karen to her friends. "That is because we are adults."

"Right," agreed Hannie and Nancy.

Obediently, I left the porch and ran into the girls' dorm where I put on socks and running shoes, and found my sun visor and a sweat shirt. Then I went to the bathroom. I had not needed to go. And I knew I would not need the sweat shirt, but I had tied the sleeves around my waist anyway. Is this how little kids feel all the time? Doing things just because some adult *tells* them to? How do kids ever become independent? I wondered, miraculously forgetting that until not long ago my father had treated me just the way the Three Musketeers were treating me.

I emerged from the cabin and announced, "Okay, I went to the bathroom. And I have a sweat shirt and a visor, and I put on socks and sneakers."

Karen eyed me critically. "All right. You're ready," she declared. "Let's go!"

"Um, Karen? I have to go to the bathroom," said Hannie sheepishly.

"Me, too," said Nancy.

"Actually, I do, too," admitted Karen.

Ten minutes later the girls and I were walking through the woods. We had taken a direction away from the secret house and secret

127

garden. We were in unexplored territory. (I made sure I could see the lake glistening through the trees to our left at all times. That way I knew we couldn't get lost.) I felt like a pioneer.

In the spirit of the game, though, I whined, "Are we almost there yet? I'm tired. My feet hurt. And I think I might have to go to the bathroom again."

The Three Musketeers giggled. And Karen said, "You know what? I don't know if we are almost there yet because I don't know where we're going."

"You don't?" I replied. I tried to sound shocked. "Well, that doesn't matter, because *I* know where we're going. We have almost reached the boat dock. Can we buy candy at the lodge? Please? Pretty please?"

"Candy! My heavens, you'll get cavities!" exclaimed Nancy.

Sure enough, the girls would not set foot in the lodge, even though they were all carrying pocket money and I knew they were dying for Neccos and root-beer barrels. Instead, we walked home by way of the docks (I was not allowed within ten feet of the edge for fear I'd fall in the lake) and the path by the water. Along the way, Nancy told me to calm down, Hannie told me to behave, and Karen reminded me to brush my teeth after lunch *and* floss them.

Later, when lunch was over and my teeth sparkled, I said to the Three Musketeers, "Okay. I did everything you said. Now will you take me swimming again?" (We had gone once after our walk.)

"Well," said Karen, "it is a little too soon after lunch. You will get cramps if you go in the water now. Besides — " (she glanced at Hannie and Nancy) " — we are tired of being the baby-sitters. We want to be the kids again."

I smiled. That was fine with me. "All right. So what do you want to do? I could read to you until you can go back in the lake."

"Well," Nancy said, "you know what we'd *really* like to do? What we'd *really* like to do is take a look at the boys' fort."

"Yeah, we have not seen it yet," said Hannie.

"Do you know where it is?" I asked.

"Sort of," said Karen. "We can find it. I don't think it is too far from our playhouse. Yesterday we could hear the boys hammering."

"Do the boys *want* you to look at their fort?"

The girls considered the question. Then Karen said, "They didn't say *not* to look at the fort. Anyway, we do not have to stay long."

"Okay," I agreed reluctantly. I was pretty sure the boys would not welcome their visitors. But as Karen had said, we didn't have to stay long.

I tramped through the woods to the secret garden with Nancy, Karen, and Hannie. From there, we listened for hammering and followed the sound until we came to . . . the fort.

"Is *that it?*" Karen whispered to me, agog.

The girls and I were standing at the edge of a clearing. Before us were David Michael, Nicky, and Linny. They were surrounded by scraps of lumber they'd found in a heap behind our cabin, a few branches and sticks of firewood, a box of nails, and several old tools. They were busily hammering some boards together. So far, the fort consisted of three boards and a tree limb hammered into a square, and something that looked like a raft.

"Hey!" shouted Hannie.

The boys looked around. "What are you doing here?" demanded David Michael.

"The girls wanted to see how your fort was coming along," I said.

"It's fine!" Nicky said crossly.

"But it isn't a fort," said Nancy. "You built a raft."

"That's a *wall*," David Michael informed her. "And it was hard to make. It took a long time."

"Is this all you've done?" asked Karen incredulously.

"First we made blueprints," Linny said.

No one believed him for a second. But no one said a word. Not until David Michael said, "Just wait. Our fort is going to be unbelievable."

I'll bet, I thought, as I led the girls out of the woods.

CHAPTER 14

Dawn

Friday

Wow! Is Shadow Lake ever
an exciting place! Okay,
maybe I'm being just a tiny
bit too perky about what I
found out today. The truth is,
I'm terrified. But that doesn't
make the lake any less
exciting. Watson, didn't you
know about Shadow Lake's
mystery? I guess not. If you
had known, you would have
told me the story (or stories)
when I asked you about the
lake during our car ride here
last Saturday. Anyway, I
like a place with a mystery.
Here's what I found out....

Hey Watson — note that Dawn has not solved the mystery. If we want an actual solved mystery (and I think we do), we better keep coming back to our cabin here. So don't get rid of it yet.

On Friday while Stacey was escaping from Sam, and Sam was pining after Stacey; and while Mary Anne was being baby-sat for by the Three Musketeers; and while David Michael, Linny, and Nicky were trying to piece together their fort, I was watching Emily Michelle and Andrew. And as usual, I was also thinking about the mystery that no doubt surrounded the lake.

Early on Friday morning, I stood by our dock with Emily and Andrew. They were already dressed in bathing suits. (Andrew's was made of a jungle-print fabric and showed a parade of animals. Emily's, a tank suit, featured a large fish blowing bubbles, and the bubbles were actually holes in the suit. Pretty cute.)

"Do you want to go swimming?" I asked the kids. "We can't go this second, but we can go in about an hour."

Andrew frowned. "Could we look at the boats again?" he wanted to know. "Claudia took us there yesterday. It was really fun. Some of the boats are decorated for the parade. I like the cowboy boat."

"You mean you want to walk to the big dock? Where the stores are?"

Andrew nodded. And Emily said clearly, "Boat."

"Sure," I said. "Good idea." Secretly, I felt relieved. I knew I was being silly, but I couldn't help thinking about the Lake Monster every time I waded into the water. And when I sat for Andrew and Emily I had to be *in* the water *with* them, since Andrew is only learning to swim, and Emily cannot swim at all. Just being *near* the lake was bad enough, considering I had actually seen the monster several times. Well, I was pretty sure I had seen him. Anyway, I liked the idea of walking to the boats.

I found T-shirts, hats, and sneakers for the kids and myself, and grabbed a little money just in case, since we would be near the stores, and we set off. We walked along the path by the lake. At first I walked between the kids, holding their hands. But they kept squirming away to examine pebbles or leaves or bugs, or to peer at the edge of the water. Finally I let them run ahead of me, as long as they stayed within view.

I listened to the water lapping at the shore. For the nine millionth time I wondered what Shadow Lake's mystery was. Everyone talked about it, but no one seemed to know details. There was the question of the shadowy monster, but there was something else, too. Something had happened a long time ago.

Suddenly an idea flashed into my brain from . . . I'm not sure where. If the mystery was old, then old people would probably know about it. I mean, old people who had lived at Shadow Lake for most of their lives. All I needed to do was find some of them and talk to them. Ask them the questions I had asked Watson.

My heart began to pound and I walked more quickly. Soon I had caught up with Andrew and Emily. Together we ran the rest of the way to the boats. Andrew stopped short when we reached the wooden dock.

"Wait till you see the dressed-up boats," he said.

"Boot!" added Emily.

"Not boot," I corrected her gently. "Boat. Say 'boat,' Emily."

"Boot."

"No. Boat."

"Boot."

Well, I thought Emily had that one wrong for the time being. But the dock was probably a great place to teach her some new vocabulary words. While Andrew examined the "dressed-up boats" again, and watched one being decorated like Disneyland, I led Emily around and pointed out objects I thought would interest her.

"Fish," I said. "Rope. Soda. Puddle. Boat."

"Boot."

I sighed. Emily could be so frustrating. She repeated all the other words properly. And anyway she had said "boat" just fine back at our cabin. Why wouldn't she say it now?

I gave up on "boat" for awhile.

Also, I remembered the mystery. I looked around. Not far away was the Disneyland boat. Andrew was watching two men put up a cardboard castle. One man looked like he was Watson's age. The other man was much older. At least seventy, I decided.

Taking Emily by the hand, I approached the boat. I shaded my eyes with my other hand. "Hello!" I called.

"Hello there!" the older man shouted back. "How do you like Snow White's castle? Could you tell it's a castle?"

"Oh, yes! It's beautiful. . . . Excuse me, sir? Could I ask you a question?"

"What's that?"

"Could I ask you a question?"

The man was cupping his hand to his ear. "Just a sec!" Slowly he climbed off the boat, found his legs (not for real; you know what I mean, don't you?) and stood in front of Emily and me. "My hearing isn't too good," he explained. "What were you saying?"

"Um, well, I'm sorry to bother you, but I wanted to ask you a question. Actually, a few questions. Do you live here at Shadow Lake?"

"In the summertime."

"Have you been coming here long?"

"Every summer since I was eight. That's over sixty years."

"Wow," I said. This was a good start. "I was wondering then. Do you know anything about the Shadow Lake mystery?"

The man frowned into the sun. He rubbed at the stubble on his chin. "Hmm. I guess you mean that story about the Bayard family. They lived here for awhile and then disappeared, or something like that. I'm not too sure."

"The Bayard family," I repeated. "Okay. Thanks a lot. Sorry I bothered you," I added. I wished I could ask him about the Lake Monster, too, but he probably wanted to get back to decorating his boat. "Good luck in the parade tomorrow!" I called as he climbed aboard.

I tore Andrew away from watching the progress on the NYC boat. "Let's look in the store," I said to him and Emily. "Maybe we can each get a treat."

"Yea!" cried Andrew.

"Treat," Emily repeated clearly.

I tried her on "boat" again.

"Boot," she said. "Boot."

"No. Boat. Oh. Make the ohhhh sound. Boa-oa-oa-oa-oat."

"Boot."

We bought ice pops at the little grocery store. (Frozfruit, actually.) The man behind the counter smiled at Emily and Andrew, then at me. Since he looked about a hundred and ten years old I boldly asked him whether he knew anything about the mystery or about the Bayards.

"Are you kidding?" said the man. "Annie Bayard was my fiancée years ago. We were going to get married. But then disaster struck."

"It *did?*" I leaned forward. "What happened? Can you tell me about the Bayards?" I whispered. "I mean, you don't have to talk about it if it's too painful or something. But I'm d — " (I almost said I was *dying* to know, but decided that might be an unfortunate choice of words.) "I'm really curious," I said instead. "I don't want to spend two weeks here without at least *try*ing to solve the mystery. I just love mysteries."

"Well, this is a good one."

The man, whose name turned out to be Stephan Weeks, said that decades and decades ago, when he was only nineteen years old, he was engaged to a beautiful eighteen-year-old girl named Annie Bayard. The Bayards were wealthy, the wealthiest family in the area, and they lived on the island out in the lake. Actually, they *owned* the little island. Their mansion was the only building on it, and they lived there year in and year out with their servants. The Bayards were a strange family. They consisted of Mr. and Mrs. Bayard, who were old, as parents go, and their children — Annie and her younger brother Ethan. That wasn't strange, but what *was* strange was that the Bayards rarely left the island. They sent the servants ashore for food and supplies. Annie and Ethan studied at home with a governess. Very few people knew the Bayards well. One who did was Stephan. He went to the island regularly to help the gardener and to make repairs in the house. That was how he had met Annie, and soon they had fallen in love.

One day, not long after Stephan had proposed to Annie, he realized that he had not seen any of the servants onshore recently, so he took a boat to the island (the Bayards had no telephone) to make sure everything was all right. And what he found was . . . nothing. Every single person who had been living on the island — the Bayards, the gardener, the servants — had vanished. The house was still there and nothing in it had been stolen or damaged. But the people were gone. And no one had any idea what happened to them. Stephan guessed that somehow they had disappeared the night before when a raging storm blew in. But how? And if they had died, where were their bodies?

"No one," Stephen said, "knows the answers to those questions. But I'll tell you something eerie. Ever since that happened, whenever a storm stirs up the lake, people around here can hear moaning and wailing, and they say they see shadows in the water. They think the lake is haunted by the spirits of Annie and her family. The island, too."

"Do you believe that?" I whispered. Stephan nodded. "What about the Lake Monster?" I couldn't help asking.

Stephan looked thoughtful. "Don't know about that," he said after a moment. "Just heard talk of it this summer. I guess stranger things have happened. But I haven't seen the monster for myself."

The kids and I had listened to Stephan for so long that by the time we left the store, we had finished our treats. I thanked Stephan and waved to him as I held the door open for Andrew and Emily. Then we began the walk home. As we passed the cowboy boat, Emily called out, "Boot!" again — and that was when I saw it. A giant cowboy boot stood at the prow of the boat.

"Oh, *that's* what you were trying to tell me!" I cried. I hugged Emily. "I see now. You're right. That is a boot."

"Boot," Emily repeated happily. Then she added, "Boot on boat."

Claudia

Satruday

Today was the day. of the boat shoe.
The parad. I finally chose a theme for
Faith Pierson and my friends and I
decrated the boat. We had to work
prety fast sinse we just started
yestruday. but we got it done and
our boat looks pretty good I think
anyway we had fun. Kristy road in
the boat with me during the parad well
she had to she knows how to drive
the boat and I dont. The parad was
fun too but on the way home we had
a scare. See Dawn was whith us then
and she thought she saw something....

Guess what I chose for the theme for *Faith Pierson*. All right, here's a clue. Dawn gave me the idea. What has been on her brain all week? (I mean, apart from the mystery.) That's right. The Lake Monster. Not that I be*lieve* in the Lake Monster (or the Loch Ness Monster or any other monster), but it seemed like a good decorating idea, and besides everyone likes to wonder about monsters (including me) even if they say they don't believe in them.

The monster idea came to me on Friday. By Friday night, my friends and I were frantically trying to fashion a monster head and a monster tail. This was not easy, since I was without my art materials, and supplies at the store were limited. (So were my funds.)

"How, exactly, are you going to turn *Faith Pierson* into a monster?" Kristy asked me on Friday evening. The seven BSC members were sitting on the dock, looking at our little boat and hoping for inspiration.

"I'm not really going to turn her *in*to a monster," I replied. "That would be too hard. Besides, we don't have enough time. I was thinking we could just make a monster head and a monster tail. We could put the head at the front of the boat, and the tail at the back of the boat. The boat itself will be the monster's body."

"What color is the Lake Monster?" Mal wanted to know.

I glanced at Dawn. "Ask Dawn," I said. "She saw the monster."

"I did n — " Dawn started to exclaim. Then she caught herself. "Green," she said. "The monster is green. And it looks like a tremendous snake."

"Maybe it really *is* a snake. Maybe that's all you saw," suggested Jessi. She shuddered. "Ew."

"I'll say. If Shadow Lake is snake-infested *and* bug-infested, I better just go on home," said Mal. "No point in staying here."

I wasn't paying much attention to the conversation. "Hmm. Green and snakelike," I muttered. "All right. Let me see. Kristy, do you think your mom would let me borrow those big green beach towels?" I asked.

"I guess so. You're not going to cut them up or anything, are you?"

"I won't even get them wet," I answered. "Well, they might get a little wet, but that's what towels are for. Okay. Now your costume, Kristy, will be easy to put — "

"My *costume?!*"

"Yes."

"I'm not wearing any costume."

"But you're going to be on the boat with me."

"I'm going to *drive* the boat, that's all."

"Kristy, if you are going to be *on* the boat *in* the parade, you have to wear a costume. That's all there is to it."

"Oh, Mom, do I really *have* to?" cried Kristy.

"Yes, dear," I replied, laughing.

"Then let me wear a boat driver's costume. You know, a sailor's hat. And epoxies or whatever those shoulder pads are called."

"Epaulets," supplied Mary Anne.

"Yeah, those."

"No, I want you to be part of the scene," I said. "I've been thinking about what we could be, and I decided you could be one of those people who lives outdoors and studies animals and stuff."

"A naturalist?" asked Stacey.

"I guess so. You could borrow Mal's hat, Kristy, and carry a pair of binoculars."

"I could also lend her a piece of my mosquito netting," offered Mal. "That would look realistic. I'll show you just how to drape it."

Kristy still looked doubtful. "What about *your* costume?" she asked me. "You better wear one. I am *not* getting dressed up if you aren't."

"Oh, I'll be dressed up. I'm going to disguise

myself as a typical tourist who wants to get close enough to the monster to photograph it."

"For that you need a costume? Why don't you just let Dawn get on the boat with us?" said Kristy, smiling.

"No, I'll have a costume. I'll wear a checked shirt and plaid shorts and I'll hang six cameras around my neck."

Reluctantly, Kristy agreed to wear her costume.

The next morning, I woke up my friends early.

"Boat parade day!" I announced. "We have work to do."

Did we ever. But with the seven of us, plus a few other pairs of helping hands, we managed to be ready for the parade by noon.

"See you later!" Kristy and I called as we climbed into *Faith Pierson*. Everyone else was walking to the boat dock to view the parade. Kristy and I were going to motor on over to the spot where the parade would start.

As soon as we reached it, I said, "Kristy, I want to go back. Now."

"Go back? We just got here."

"I know, but I decided I can't go through with this."

"Oh, no. Why not?"

"Because you and Charlie and everyone were right. *Faith Pierson* doesn't belong in the parade. She's too little. All the other boats really are yachts or houseboats or something big. No one's even going to be able to *see* us. Besides, our decorations are puny."

My lake monster consisted of a snaky green monster head made from a couple of rolled-up beach towels, and a green monster tail made from more towels. Their only interesting feature was that they could move. I'd rigged them so that if I pulled on wires, they bobbed up and down. In all honesty, they looked fairly realistic. But in case someone wasn't sure what they represented, I had made a sign for the side of the boat which read THE LAKE MONSTER. (It was the second sign I had made. The first one said THE LACK MUNSTER, but Kristy had seen it and caught my mistakes in time.)

"Come on, Kristy, let's turn the boat around," I said.

"No way. We came this far. Anyway, Mary Anne and Stacey and Mom and everyone are at the dock now, waiting for us to go by. If we don't show up, they'll think something horrible happened, like we capsized and were eaten by . . . the Lake Monster."

I had to smile at that. "All right," I said. "I'll risk it."

We were in the parade lineup by that time. Ahead of us was the boat with the western theme. Behind us was the Mardi Gras boat. Kristy started *Faith Pierson*'s motor. She kept it on low as we made our way slowly through the water in the direction of the dock. A few people were watching from the path by the shore. They clapped and cheered for the boats in front of us. Then they clapped and cheered for the cowboy boat.

We were the next attraction. Just don't laugh at us, I pleaded silently.

They didn't! *Faith Pierson* received a big round of applause.

"They *like* us!" I exclaimed.

"Why not?" Kristy replied. "I think we're pretty cute."

By the time we reached the big dock I was used to looking out at the shore, waving the monster's head and tail around, and listening for clapping and cheers. I thought I heard one person call out, "Gutsy!" (It sounded like a compliment.)

"What does gutsy mean?" I asked Kristy.

"It means that what we did takes guts. We have courage."

"Yes!" I agreed. I was no longer afraid of the crowd on the dock.

Guess what. Not only did the crowd love

us, but we won a prize when the parade was over. And it was not one of those situations in which everyone wins a prize for something. No. Only four awards were given out, and Kristy and *Faith Pierson* and I received a ribbon that said MOST SPIRIT. Kristy told me I could keep it, and I knew I would — forever.

The parade had ended, but the excitement hadn't. On the way back to the cabin we had a real scare. Kristy was driving the boat again, and I was sitting in the front with Dawn who had come aboard to see our ribbon and then had decided to ride home with us.

Most of the bigger boats were going to stay at the dock, so by the time we were halfway to our cabin, we had the lake nearly to ourselves. Kristy was concentrating on piloting the boat, I was daydreaming, and Dawn was gazing across the water at the island.

Suddenly she screamed. And I mean *screamed*. I jumped a mile and Kristy jerked the steering wheel to the left.

"What is *wrong?"* cried Kristy.

"I see the Lake Monster for real!" Dawn replied, pointing.

I looked at the lake and saw nothing but a few teensy waves.

CHAPTER 16

Kristy

Sunday

Today was the beginning of our big adventure. I have to admit that when Dawn told us the story about the Bayards and the island and Shadow Lake, I almost changed my mind about our boat trip. (So did everyone else.) But in the end, I was able to listen to reason. Besides, I wanted to experience as much about the lake as possible, Watson. I wanted to be able to say to you," Here's another cool thing about our summer place. We can go out to the little island for a picnic or for a camping adventure. There is so much to do here!"

Unfortunately, not everyone was quite as enthusiastic about our outing as I was. Dawn was particularly not enthusiastic.

"You must be crazy, Kristy," she said. "You're not playing with a full deck. You're a few bricks short of a load. The lights are on, but no one's at home. You are — "

"I get the picture," I said. "Look, Dawn, if you don't want to come with us you don't have to. You can stay here."

"Wait, can I say just one more thing?"

"Be my guest."

"The cheese has slipped off the cracker."

I giggled. "Okay. You have established that you think I'm — "

"Looney tunes," supplied Dawn.

"Stop it! Geez, for someone who's terrified, you're sure, um, jolly."

"I pride myself on retaining my sense of humor. Even under duress."

At this point, Claudia nudged me. "*What did she say?*"

"I'm not sure. I think she's covering up her fear of . . . the island," I replied. I hummed a few bars from the theme music for *The Twilight Zone.*

"Okay, okay, okay," said Dawn. She collapsed onto a lower bunk. My friends and I were clustered in the girls' bedroom, which was a big mess.

We were packing for our overnight trip to the island. To Shadow Island, as Dawn now called it. But anyone would have thought we were going to spend a month there instead of just a night. We planned to be on the island for less than twenty-four hours. Apparently, a few of us had forgotten that. Others (one in particular) had kept that in mind and still thought we were crazy to go to the island even for five minutes.

It was Sunday morning. My friends and I had decided to leave for Shadow Island right after lunch. I was going to drive *Faith Pierson* there. (I just love saying I was going to *drive*.) Unfortunately, *Faith Pierson* was not big enough to hold all seven BSC members, so I was going to take three of us, and Sam was going to borrow a boat from the people in the cabin just up the lake (our next-shore neighbors) and drive the three remaining club members to the island. Then he was going to leave us (and *Faith Pierson*) there and come back at noon on Monday.

"Stacey?" I said. "How come you're packing your purse into your knapsack?" I asked, watching her stuff the strap down. "I don't think Shadow Island features any shops."

Stacey made a face at me. "I'm protecting my privacy. I'm afraid Sam will go through my purse if I leave it here."

"Oh, he will not," I said. "Sam's a goofball, but he isn't a snoop."

"Okay." Stacey unpacked her pocketbook.

I looked around the room. Jessi was packed and ready to go. She was sitting demurely on a bed, ankles crossed, waiting. Actually, she was staring into space, lost in thought. Claud was emptying her makeup bag into a pocket in her knapsack.

"Planning on going out tonight?" Dawn asked her. "Got a hot date with a ghost? Old Mr. Bayard maybe?"

Claud looked a little sheepish. "I guess I don't *really* need this stuff."

"Well, I'm ready!" Mary Anne spoke up.

"I can't believe you're so relaxed about this," Dawn said to her.

"It's because I don't believe in ghosts," replied Mary Anne boldly. Then she added in a whisper, "Anyway I don't think I do."

Dawn stared at her. Then she turned suddenly, dove for her knapsack, and started to unpack it. "I've just made a decision," she announced. "I've decided I'm not going to Shadow Island after all."

"Oh, good," I said. "You can stay here and

have a sleepover party with Emily Michelle and the Three Musketeers."

"Hmm. Maybe I'll come with you after all."

"Is everyone ready?" I asked my friends. "Why don't you stand by the door with your stuff so I can make sure everything will fit into the bo — "

I stopped speaking. I stared rudely at Mal. I couldn't help it. "Mallory, does all that stuff belong to you?" She was surrounded by, like, seven tote bags.

"Yup."

"What on earth did you pack?"

"Well . . . a nightshirt, a T-shirt, my toothbrush, the mosquito netting, two hats, mosquito spray, tick spray, general bug spray — "

"Who's General Bug?" interrupted Jessi.

" — a dozen citronella candles, calamine lotion, Lava soap, first-aid cream, drying lotion, Q-tips, cotton balls, spider repellent, and . . . and I'm not leaving any of it behind. Who knows what insects will be out on that island. It could be over*run* with creepy-crawlies. It could be in*fested*."

"Okay. I changed my mind again. I'm *not* going," said Dawn.

"Slumber party," I reminded her.

"Oh, yeah. Coming after all."

* * *

Around one-thirty that afternoon my friends and I finished loading up *Faith Pierson* and the other boat, the *Lake Mist*.

"Oh, my lord," muttered Dawn.

"Slumber party," I whispered, and she kept quiet.

Into *Lake Mist* climbed Jessi, Mal, and Mary Anne. Sam was at the helm. "Um, I can take one more, I think," he said, glancing at Stacey. "Room for one more."

"No, you have four," I told my brother, "and so do I. The boats are even this way. Claud, Stacey, and Dawn are coming with me."

Stacey shot me this incredibly grateful look, while Sam, the picture of disappointment, took the wheel of *Lake Mist*. I felt bad for him, but I didn't want to start our adventure by making Stacey angry.

On the dock were gathered Mom, Watson, my brothers, the Three Musketeers, Nicky, Linny, Emily, and Nannie. I felt as if they were seeing us off on a cruise.

I felt like a celebrity.

I also felt quite grown-up. That is, until Watson called Sam back to the dock, looking awfully serious.

"Yeah?" said Sam, scrambling out of *Lake Mist*.

"Would you kind of check out the island before you leave the girls there?" he said. (He was not exactly whispering. Also, he said "the girls" as if he *meant* "the children.")

I bristled. I was all set to stand up and say, "We are *not* babies, Watson," when I felt Claud's hand on my arm. "Chill out," she whispered.

I chilled.

Anyway, I guess Watson had a point. None of us knew a thing about the island. It could easily have been the headquarters for a gang of thieves and thugs. Or it could have been overrun with poisonous plants. Who knew?

When Sam finally returned to *Lake Mist* I looked at the crowd on the dock. For one brief, scary moment I thought my mother was going to cry, but she held herself together nicely.

" 'Bye!" I called.

"Have fun," said Mom bravely.

"Be careful, Mal!" said Nicky.

"I will!"

"Sam's coming back for us at noon tomorrow," I reminded everyone. "But if anything should happen, *Faith Pierson* will be with us. We can always come ashore if we need to. Or four of us can."

157

"Use good judgment," said Watson, like I really planned to rely on a poor sense of judgment while my friends and I were alone on an unfamiliar, possibly haunted island.

A few minutes later we were off. We sailed leisurely away from our dock. (Well, we didn't *sail*, technically, but you know what I mean.)

"Shadow Island, here we come," whispered Dawn.

"*Fun*, here we come," I said pointedly.

"Aughhh!" shrieked Dawn.

I didn't bother to turn away from the wheel. "Dawn, the island may be haunted, but our boat isn't."

"Aughhh!" shrieked Stacey.

"What's going on?" I asked.

"Turn around," said Claud, giggling.

I turned around — just in time to see Dawn get hit with a stream of water. It came from *Lake Mist*. Jessi had shot her with a water pistol.

"Take the wheel," I said to Stacey, grinning.

"I don't know how to — "

"Just hold it!" I cried. Then I leaned over, scooped up some lake water, and shot it back at Jessi, using only my hands. (Sam taught me

how to do that. I have pretty good aim.)

The rest of the trip across the lake was one big water fight. By the time the boats were approaching the island, most of us were soaked.

"There it is," Dawn said, and the water fight came to an end.

"It doesn't *look* haunted," I said brightly.

No one answered. I glanced at *Lake Mist*, which Sam was steering alongside *Faith Pierson*. Everyone on board was scoping out the island. Several minutes later we were wading ashore. We grounded the boats.

"Okay, let's take a look around," said Sam.

From up close, the island appeared quite a bit larger than I'd first imagined it would be. Of course, the Bayards had actually lived there, had built a mansion there. The house was gone now, Dawn had said, but still. . . .

"I think it's pretty," said Mallory. "It's so green."

"I like the pebbly beach," added Mary Anne.

"It's hard to imagine that an entire family disappeared from here," whispered Dawn.

CHAPTER 17

Mallory ⚓

Sunday

Sam stayed with us while we explored the island.
I was kind of glad he did. I didn't want to
admit it, but I was a little scared — just a little —
because of what Dawn had told us about the
Bayards. But the island is wonderful. Really,
Watson. It's beautiful and it's fun to explore.
It would be a great place for picnics. You
could spend a day here fishing and swimming
and climbing rocks and hiking and eating....

Mallory
☺

"I like the island. I really do," I said as Sam and my friends and I took our first look around. The island was . . . well, it was clean. Shadow Lake sparkled around it, the pebbles and small rocks on the shore gleamed in the sun, and the leaves on the trees glistened a bright green. We could hear the water lapping against the rocks and some crickets chirping, but that was about it.

Crickets. I began to wonder about the insect situation. While my friends scrambled over the rocks, I removed several of my tote bags from *Lake Mist*. I exchanged my sun visor for one of my hats. Then I searched around for the mosquito netting. I wasn't going to go anywhere *near* the woods unless I was fully protected.

"Mallory, come on!" called Jessi from the line of trees bordering the shore. "Sam wants to get going."

"Okay!" I ran forward a few yards, then skidded to a stop. What were we supposed to do with our gear? And who was going to watch the boats? We couldn't just leave our things while we ran off to . . . Oh, yeah. No one else is on the island, I reminded myself. At least, no one we know of. We could leave anything anywhere we wanted. (And if something disappeared, that would be a clue that *we* should leave, too.)

I caught up with my friends who had decided to check out the shore first, by walking around the island.

"Boy, this is a beautiful place," I said as we tramped along.

"Yeah," agreed Dawn. "But you know what? I can't stop thinking about the Bayards. How could an entire family disappear, along with their maids and the gardener and everyone?"

Claud shrugged her shoulders. "That's what makes the mystery intriguing."

"What happened to their house, Dawn?" I asked. "Why isn't it here?"

"I'm not sure. Stephan just said it was gone. He was in the middle of the story and I didn't want to interrupt him. It was probably torn down."

"Oh, you know — Ow!" I squawked.

"What's the matter?" asked Sam.

"Something bit me."

"*Again?*" said Kristy.

I stuck out my tongue at her. "Yes, again. And it felt like a tick."

"Mal, how on earth do you know how it feels to be bitten by a tick? You can't feel tick bites. I mean, not until after you've gotten them and they're irritated and everything," said Kristy.

"Thank you, Dr. Spock," I replied.

"Mallory, put some calamine lotion on it and let's keep going," said Sam, turning to face me. He was several yards ahead, hiking along with a large stick he'd found. "I want to get back before the entire day is shot."

What a grouch. Oh, well.

I reached obediently into my knapsack and emerged with one of my bottles of lotion. I stopped, sat down, and applied some lotion to the bite with a Q-tip. Then I replaced the bottle carefully.

"Ready?" asked Sam, and I nodded.

We walked all the way around the island. We didn't stop until we had returned to the boats and our gear. We had not noticed one sign of any other people. No litter, no campfires, no shouts or calls, not even a footprint anywhere. Sam took a quick tour through the woods and decided the island was safe for us BSC members. Then he put *Lake Mist* back in the water and climbed in.

"See you tomorrow!" Kristy called.

"With any luck," Sam replied. (I think he was hiding a smile.) Then he added, "Stacey, dahling, *do* enjoy yourself." He turned away before he could see the face she made.

For a moment, my friends and I stood where we were and just gazed after Sam as he motored away.

"He did not investigate the woods thoroughly at *all*," said Dawn.

"If any ghosts are in there you don't think they'd walk up and introduce themselves, do you?" Claud asked her.

"I guess not."

"Boy, this is kind of like *Gilligan's Island*," spoke up Mary Anne.

"Hey, yeah!" agreed Jessi. "Let's see. How does that song go?"

"Like this!" I exclaimed. "Come and listen to a story 'bout a man named Jed, a poor mountaineer barely kept his — "

"No!" cried Kristy, giggling. "That's *The Beverly Hillbillies*!"

KER-RASH!

"Aughhh!" screamed the seven of us. And Dawn added, "It's Mr. Bayard! His spirit is here!"

We were about to become hysterical when Kristy said, "Wait a second. That wasn't any ghost. This branch just fell down. See?"

Everyone believed the fallen branch theory except for Dawn.

"How do you know?" she shrieked.

"Because it wasn't here a minute ago."

"Oh."

"Come on, you guys. Let's set up our camp. Then we can *really* explore the island. Maybe," Kristy added, glancing at Dawn, "we'll find some clues that will solve the mystery."

"I was hoping to solve it from a distance," said Dawn. "Not with Mr. Bayard's ghost looking over my shoulder."

"Well, you're here now," snapped Kristy. I could tell she was fed up with Dawn. "Let's get going."

Our camp was not very elaborate. We were going to slumber away in sleeping bags under the stars. (We had brought along two tents, but we didn't plan to put them up unless rain threatened.) So we piled our sleeping bags on the shore and then cleared an area for a campfire. We lined the circle with rocks and gathered dry sticks and twigs from the woods. Finally we stowed our gear in the shade.

"Okay, let's explore!" said Kristy, and, like ducklings, the rest of us followed her into the woods.

"What are we looking for?" asked Jessi, a few minutes later.

"Nothing," answered Dawn pointedly.

"Adventure," said Kristy.

We walked along in silence.

Several *more* minutes later, Claud said, "I don't see anything but trees."

"And rocks," said Stacey.

"And bricks," I added.

"Bricks! What are bricks doing on the island?" screeched Dawn. "Bricks are man-made. They aren't natural. Someone has been here!"

"Of course someone's been here. The ghosts of the Bayards," said Kristy.

Kristy was laughing. She was teasing Dawn. But as it turned out, she wasn't far from the truth. Claud and Jessi immediately ran for the bricks and even before the rest of us had caught up with them, Claudia was exclaiming, "Oh, my lord!"

"What?" screamed Dawn.

"I think we just found the Bayards' house. Or what's left of it."

That did it. Every one of us, even Dawn, dashed headlong to the spot where Claud and Jessi were now crouching.

"Claud's right," whispered Jessi. "Look at this."

I knelt down next to her. I picked up a piece of scorched brick. I looked around. Bricks, all of them scorched, stretched away from me in two jagged lines. The lines were at right angles to each other and met near where my friends and I were clustered.

"I think," I said, whispering, too, "that this is the foundation to some building that burned down. It must have been the Bayards' house."

We were quiet for several seconds. Then we all began talking at once.

"You mean the house *burned* down?" said Kristy.

"I thought the Bayards disappeared during a storm," said Mary Anne.

"They did, but their house didn't," said Dawn, frowning.

"I wonder if the Bayards even know their house burned down," mused Stacey. "They might not, you know. I mean, if they're still alive."

"I bet their *spirits* know," said Dawn. "Spirits usually know about awful things like that. And I bet they're mad. They probably roam around and haunt the island, just like they haunt the lake. I *told* you guys the island was haunted."

"Dawn, you are jumping to conclusions," said Mary Anne. But her hands were shaking and her voice was trembling.

"Hey, where are you going?" called Kristy.

"Back to our stuff," said Dawn. "We're moving."

"We're what?" I shouted.

"We're moving. We are much too close to these ruins. I'm not spending the night with this ghost-house right next to me."

"*Dawn!*" yelped Kristy.

But Mary Anne said, "Maybe she's right. . . ."

"You *guys!*" Kristy stamped her foot. The rest of us were following Dawn, though, so Kristy trailed after us. By the time she reached the shore, each of us was grabbing a sleeping bag. And I was juggling my bags of insect artillery. I did have an awful lot of gear.

"Do you *really* want to rebuild our campfire?" Kristy asked us.

I glanced at the neat circle of stones which had taken half an hour to arrange, and at the sticks which had taken even longer to collect. Then I glanced at my friends. And then I glanced across the lake.

"I see him!" I yelled at the top of my lungs. "I see the monster! He's out there. And he's — "

"Mal, what are you looking at?" asked Claudia.

"That . . . that . . ." I shaded my eyes. "That tree branch," I said, letting out my breath. "Oops. It was a tree branch. Never mind."

By the time we'd recovered from that trauma, and I had reapplied my insect repellent, nobody felt like moving camp. So we stayed put. We began to fix dinner, which consisted of canned stuff, fruit, and junk food. We lit our fire and ate supper contentedly. Dawn insisted on facing the woods, in order to spot danger immediately, but that was okay with us.

We barely noticed when darkness began to fall.

Dawn

Sunday Night and
Monday Morning

Mal may not have noticed
when it started to get dark, but
I did. This was because the
first time I saw a firefly I
thought it was the eye of
a ghost in the woods. Luckily
I kept that thought to
myself.

I have spent other nights
sleeping on islands, but not
haunted islands. Not islands
full of vengeful ghosts who

Dawn, cut that out. The island
was perfectly fine. I was

I know that, Kristy. You
didn't let me finish. Watson,
my night on the island was
scary only because of the

story about the Bayards. Which may be true. Who knows? The important thing was that the next morning, all six of my friends and I were still in one piece. We had survived. And I had found a secret souvenir.

Wink, wink. Wink, wink.

I was huddled by our campfire, facing the woods. I was sitting in the same position in which I'd been sitting since we'd eaten supper. And something was winking at me from the dark beyond the trees. I almost screamed, "Ghost eyes! The Bayards are here!" Then one of those ghost eyes flew in front of my face and winked on and off.

It was a firefly, a lightning bug. And so were those other ghost eyes.

I relaxed. (Just a smidge.)

Our supper was over. Everyone except Stacey and me had eaten canned baked beans, apples, potato chips, and s'mores. Stacey and I had eaten the beans, the apples, and some stoned wheat thins, and later I had also eaten a slice of watermelon. (Guess what. When my brother Jeff was little he used to say "water-lemon.") Not a bad supper, all things considered.

Now the seven of us were sitting around the fire. Claud, Kristy, and Mal were *still* making and eating s'mores.

"You guys are going to get sick," said Stacey, eyeing them nervously. (She absolutely cannot stand to see, or hear, anyone puke.)

"Nah," said Kristy. "Once I ate four s'mores, large ones, and nothing happened except that Mom got mad because I'd used up the graham crackers."

We sat in silence for a few minutes. I shivered. The night air on the island was cooler than it was on the mainland. As if she were reading my mind, Jessi said, "Brrr. I'm freezing." She was already wearing jeans, a long-sleeved T-shirt, and a sweater. Now she pulled a sweatshirt on over the sweater and edged closer to our fire.

I shivered again. "You know," I said, "sometimes when a ghost is hanging around, the temperature drops." I happen to know quite a bit about ghosts. I read about them constantly. And personally, I think a ghost lives in the secret passage at my house. (The house is centuries old, and the passage used to be part of the Underground Railroad which helped slaves escape from the South to safety in the North.)

Kristy rolled her eyes at me. "The temperature also drops," she said, "when you're on an island in the middle of a lake and it's almost nighttime." She popped the last bite of her s'more into her mouth.

"Well, anyway," said Mary Anne, "you guys have to admit that Shadow Island *is* a little spooky."

"Yeah," agreed Mal, whose back was to the woods. She turned around and stared into the trees. "I wonder what really happened to the Bayards."

"You know what I think is the strangest part of the story?" asked Jessi. "That *every*one on the island disappeared — the Bayards *plus* the gardener *plus* the maids, or whoever their servants were. If just the Bayards had vanished, I would think maybe the family was in trouble and they wanted to disappear. But then they wouldn't bring along their *gard*ener and everyone. So there must have been some kind of natural disaster."

"But nothing had happened to the mansion," I pointed out. "Not right then."

"Yeah," said Stace. "A storm would have damaged the house."

"*I* want to know when the house burned down," said Mary Anne.

"I think that's one thing we can find out," I told her. "I'm sure Stephan knows. He just didn't mention it because he got so caught up in the story about the night the Bayards vanished. Boy, I sure would love to solve *that* mystery. All those missing people."

"Somehow the mystery seems scarier when it's *un*solved," said Jessi. "The weird possibilities are endless."

"Maybe," said Claudia, lowering her voice so we had to lean toward her to hear her, "a maniac sailed to the island in the dead of night and murdered everyone he could find."

"What did he do with the bodies?" I challenged her.

"Buried them?"

"He must have been an awfully tidy killer. No bloodstains anywhere," I said. "Nothing out of place in the house, no furniture turned over."

"Oh, yeah."

Mallory frowned slightly. "You know," she said, "I've read plenty of stories, *true* stories, about regular, everyday people who were abducted by aliens and put aboard spacecrafts for science experiments or something. Most of them were returned to earth, but maybe the people on the island were whisked off to some other planet." Mal glanced around at our faces in the firelight. "Well, it *could* have happened!"

"We didn't say anything," I said.

"I know, but you were going to. Anyway, that theory is just as reasonable as any other one. I was watching this TV show once — "

"SHHH!" I hissed suddenly.

"*Dawn*," Mal protested.

"SHHH!" I hissed again. "I heard something."

Everyone became silent. We didn't hear a thing.

"What did it sound like, Dawn?" Claudia whispered.

"Like someone walking around in the woods."

"Oh, my lord."

The seven of us listened for a few more moments. Nothing.

"It was probably a squirrel or a rabbit," said Mary Anne.

"Probably," I replied, but I didn't believe that for a second.

Slowly we began to talk about other things — the boat show, the dance . . . Sam.

"He really likes you, Stace," I said.

"How do you know?"

I shrugged. "I can just tell, that's all."

The longer we talked the darker the night became and the sleepier we felt. My eyes began to swim. "I think it's bedtime," I murmured and, fully clothed, I slid inside my sleeping bag. " 'Night, you guys."

"Good night," they replied.

The next thing I knew I was waking sleepily. The fire had died to a dim glow. Above me, the sky was black and the stars shone fiercely. Clearly, it was not yet morning. But I could hear whispered voices.

I raised myself onto one elbow and thought I could make out Mary Anne on the other side of the campfire. She was gesturing to Claudia.

"What's going on?" I murmured.

Mary Anne and Claud jumped a mile. "We saw something in the woods," Mary Anne answered. "Something whitish. And wispy."

Next to me, Mallory sat up and squealed, "You saw a *ghost?*"

That did it. Pandemonium. In three seconds, the seven of us were wide awake and scrambling out of our sleeping bags.

"I want to go back!" cried Mary Anne.

"I'm coming with you!" added Jessi.

"You guys, it's two o'clock in the morning!" said Kristy. "I can't take us across the lake *now*. It wouldn't be safe."

"But this is an emergency!" I exclaimed. "If I had appendicitis, you'd take me back no matter what time it was."

Kristy looked thoughtful. "Well," she said slowly, "the boat can only hold four people. That is its absolute limit. So who's going to stay behind?"

In answer, everyone except Kristy made a dash for the boat. When we turned around, we saw Kristy still standing by the campfire amid our rumpled sleeping bags. I think she was smiling.

I began to laugh. "This is ridiculous," I said. "Come on, everybody. Let's go back to sleep."

My friends and I returned to our camp. We crawled into our sleeping bags and we fell asleep. Well, I assume the others fell asleep. At any rate, they became very quiet, their breathing deep and even.

But not I. I was awake for the rest of the night. I remained on Ghost Alert until I could see the first rays of sunshine on the horizon. I smiled. We had survived the night.

I sat up and gazed into the woods. I saw nothing but trees and rocks and ferns. I heard nothing but birds and insects. I sighed with relief. The woods seemed so peaceful that I decided to investigate them again. I tiptoed away from our campfire and into the cool early morning smells of damp earth and awakening plants. I walked in the same direction we had walked the night before, and soon I reached the crumbling foundation of the Bayards' house. I sat down on a pile of bricks.

The walls (what was left of them) stretched away in different directions, intersecting bits of other walls, sometimes dwindling to nothing. The Bayards' house must have been *huge*, I decided.

I leaned over to examine the bricks — and my eyes fell on something gold gleaming at my feet. Whatever it was, I had nearly stepped on it. I picked up a very old, very fragile locket. It was shaped like a heart. Carefully I opened it. Nothing was inside, but when I closed it again I noticed the initials engraved on one side. AB in fancy script. Annie Bayard? Maybe. Probably. I just had a feeling about it. Often, my feelings are right. I decided the locket had appeared to me as a sign; a sign to let me know the Bayards' spirits existed and to thank me for believing in them. The locket had not been there the day before. I was sure of that. If it had been, one of us would have seen it. It wasn't hidden at all.

So. It had appeared during the night. Had it appeared after Mary Anne and Claud had seen the whitish, wispy thing in the woods? I decided that was probably another question I'd never be able to answer. I added it to the Bayard Mystery, the Shadow Lake Mystery.

Later that day, Sam arrived in *Lake Mist*, and the members of the BSC left the island. We motored safely to shore, and spent the afternoon telling everyone about our adventures. At one point, I snuck off for the boat dock and found Stephan in his grocery store. I asked him when the Bayards' house had burned down.

"One year to the day after they disappeared," he told me. "No one knows how the fire started."

Then I gave him the locket I'd found. "This is for you," I said. "It's from Annie."

DAVID MICHAEL

WENSDAY

TODAY LINNY AND NICKY AND I
WHERE WORKING ON THE FORT.
AGAIN. IT IS ALMOST FINISHED I
GUESS. I WAS HAPPY ABOUT OUR
FORTE BUT THEN SOMETHING BAD
HAPPENED. I COULD NOT FIND
SHANNON ANYWHERE SHE HAD BEEN
IN THE WOODS WITH US AND I
CALLED FOR HER BUT SHE DIDNT
COME. OH NO! I SAID. MY PUPPY
IS GONE !!!!

Wednesday was really, really scary. Well, not the whole day. Just the part when Shannon was gone.

My friends and I had worked on our fort almost every day. It was looking good. We had built two walls and nailed them to trees. (The Three Musketeers saw one of the walls. They called it a raft. What do girls know about building stuff?) Now Linny was building a third wall while Nicky and I tried to figure out how to make windows and a door. If we just put up four walls our fort would be a dark box with no way in or out. Nicky was *supposed* to be helping Linny with the walls since they were a bigger job, but he and Linny could not work on the same thing without fighting most of the time.

Nicky and Linny and I had started working on our fort very early on Wednesday morning. We had eaten breakfast by ourselves. I was proud of us. We had remembered to eat Pop-Tarts *and* orange Popsicles. That was almost as good as having fruit and orange juice. Plus, we had eaten toast, cereal, and bagels. That was a very balanced meal. And we had only left a small mess in the kitchen. I did not think anyone would notice the milk that had dripped off the table. Anyway, Boo-Boo would probably come along and lap it up.

As soon as we had scooped most of the spilled Froot Loops back into the box, Linny and Nicky and I found our tools. Then I called for Shannon. Since everyone else was asleep I had to call her very softly. "Shannon, Shannon. Here, girl." I was just whispering, but Shannon heard me. She ran to me. Her toenails clicked on the kitchen floor, but she did not bark or whine. "Good girl," I said. "Okay, let's go."

When we were in the woods we could talk in our regular voices.

"Only three more days to work on the fort, you guys," I said. I could hardly believe our vacation was almost over.

Linny was thinking the same thing. "I have never been away with someone else's family for such a long time," he said. "Two whole weeks. Before, that seemed like forever. Now Saturday is almost here."

"The boat show is over," I said. "My sister's campout is over. She spent the night on that island — and saw a ghost."

"No, she didn't!" cried Linny.

"Well, she might have," said Nicky.

"You don't believe in ghosts, do you?" Linny asked Nicky. He was walking on one side of me. Nicky was walking on the other side. Linny had to lean around me in order to see Nicky.

"I have *seen* a ghost," replied Nicky.

"Oh, you have not."

"Have so."

"Was it Casper the Friendly Ghost?"

"Cut it out, you guys!" I exclaimed. Then I realized I could not see Shannon, so I whistled for her. From up ahead she barked. And when we reached the clearing, guess who we found. Shannon. She was sitting in our fort. Well, she was sitting in the corner where the two walls met.

"Good girl! Good girl, Shannon!" I cried. "Okay. You can play while Linny and Nicky and I build." Shannon stood up. She shook herself. Then she frisked into the trees.

"Hey, David Michael," said Linny, "I'm tired of working on the walls. Can't I help you with the windows?"

"*I'm* helping him with the windows," Nicky answered.

"We don't need three people working on windows," I said. "We don't even need two. But two people could work on the walls."

"Okay, let's switch. You and Nicky work on the walls, and I will work on the windows," said Linny.

"Why don't you and *Nicky* work on the walls?"

"NO!" exclaimed Linny and Nicky.

"Geez. All right," I said. "I'll help you with the walls, Linny."

"No fair!" said Nicky.

I looked at my watch. "We are wasting time. If we want to win our bet with the girls we better start working."

We went to work. But nobody was talking. All I could hear was *pound, pound, pound.* Once, when no one was hammering, I heard voices. Karen and Nancy and Hannie were playing in their playhouse.

"Where is Shannon?" asked Nicky suddenly.

I looked up. I listened. No Shannon. I had not seen her for awhile. "Hey, Shannon!" I yelled. "Shannon! Here, girl!" I waited for the sound of Shannon crashing through the bushes. (She is not usually very quiet. I do not think she could sneak up on anything.) But I did not hear any crashing. I did not even hear any rustling. "Shannon!" I called again.

"She's probably visiting the girls," said Nicky. "I'll go check."

When Nicky came back, he was not with Shannon. "The girls have not seen her all morning," he reported.

187

"Then I'll check out the cabin," I said. "Maybe she got confused and went home. Or maybe she was hungry. Hey, did we feed Shannon her breakfast?"

Nicky and Linny paused to think. "You know what? We forgot," said Linny.

"Did not!" said Nicky.

"Did too!"

"See you guys later. I am going back to the house," I announced.

I looked in every room in our cabin. I even looked in the bathrooms. No Shannon. I ran out the front door to the dock. Kristy was wading in the lake with Andrew and Emily. Claudia and Stacey were diving off the dock. But Shannon was not there.

I was starting to feel nervous.

I ran back through the woods to our fort. By the time I got there, I was panting. "You — " (pant) " — guys!" I exclaimed. "Did Shannon — " (pant) " — come back?"

Linny and Nicky glanced at each other.

"No," said Nicky. "We thought you would find her at the cabin."

I shook my head. "Nope. Not there. I looked really carefully. I looked down on our dock, too. Why doesn't she come when I call?"

"Let's all look," said Linny, jumping to his feet.

Linny and Nicky and I called and whistled. We ran through the woods.

No Shannon.

"Oh, no!" I cried. "She's gone."

"No, she is not," said Nicky and Linny together.

"Then she's hurt and she can't move."

"If she is hurt, we will find her," said Nicky.

"Yeah," agreed Linny.

"How?" I asked.

Silence. Then Linny said, "Well, we will organize — "

" — a search party!" Nicky finished his sentence.

"Right!" said Linny. "Let's go get the girls."

"No, you get the girls," said Nicky. "I will find Kristy and her friends. David Michael, you find your mom and everyone else."

"Then we will spread out, and look for Shannon," added Linny. "And we will not stop looking until we find her." He dashed through the trees. "Hey, you girls!" he shouted. "Hannie! Karen! Nancy!"

Nicky and I took off for the cabin. "Kristy is at the dock," I told Nicky. "So are Claudia and Stacey. I bet they know where Mom is." We ran to the cabin. We ran in the back door and out the front door. We ran onto the dock.

We were running so fast we had trouble stopping. We almost clobbered Stacey.

"Hey, you two, what's going on?" she said.

"Shannon's missing!" I exclaimed. "Kristy, where's Mom?"

"Down by the boats with Watson and Nannie."

"Thanks!"

In half an hour everybody was standing by our fort. Even Emily Michelle. Even Nannie. And even some new friends of Jessi's named Daniel and Bridget. Now that everyone was there, I was not sure what to do. That didn't matter. Nicky and Linny took over.

"One big person has to go with each kid," said Nicky.

"Half of us should look in the woods," added Linny, "and some should look by the lake, and the rest should look by the stores."

I was beginning to feel an awful lump in my throat. I was afraid we would never see Shannon again. I tramped through the woods with Watson. "Shannon! Shannon!" we called.

"Yip! Yip-yip-yip!"

"I hear her! I hear her, Watson!" I cried.

And soon Shannon trotted over to us. She was not hurt.

"I guess she was just having a good time," I said.

190

Nicky and Linny and I called off the search. Then we went back to work on the fort. This time, I sawed boards for the door, and Nicky and Linny finished that third wall. "Good work!" they told each other.

And I added, "You guys are heroes."

CHAPTER 20

KAREN

FRIDAY

BOO, BOO, BOO, BOO. TOMORROW
WE HAVE TO GO HOME. I DO NOT
WANT TO GO YET. I AM NOT
READY. NOBODY ELSE IS EITHER.
DADDY, CAN'T WE STAY AT SHADOW
LAKE FOR JUST ONE MORE WEEK?
PLEEEEEEASE? I WILL NEVER
ASK FOR ANYTHING ELSE AGAIN IN
MY WHOLE LIFE. I PROMISE. OH,
EXCEPT FOR ONE THING. CAN WE
STOP FOR ICE CREAM ON THE WAY
HOME?

Hee, hee, hee. You will *never* guess what happened on Friday. I saw it myself and I still do not believe it.

"Today," I said to Hannie and Nancy, "the boys have to finish their fort. And we get to see if it is better than our playhouse."

"It won't be," said Hannie.

"How come?" asked Nancy.

"Because Linny is working on it."

My friends and I giggled.

"Well, I cannot wait," I said. "I will not have to do a single chore for the rest of the summer. And when David Michael goes back to school in September he will write a composition that starts, 'On my summer vacation I just did chores. All my chores and all Karen's chores.' "

"Let's go to the fort *now!*" cried Nancy.

The Three Musketeers had been sitting by the secret garden. Now we jumped to our feet. We ran through the woods.

"Yoo-hoo! Yoo-hoo, boys!" I called. I began to laugh.

My friends called, "Yoo-hoo!" with me. They laughed, too.

I heard my brother groan. Then I heard Nicky say, "Here they come." I know he meant us girls.

"Okay, you guys," I said. Nancy and Hannie and I were facing Nicky and Linny and David Michael. "This is it. Last day. Time for our bet. Is your fort better than our playhouse?" I peered around the boys at their fort. I started to laugh again. "I do *not* think so!" I went on. "Our playhouse is much better."

"Prove it!" said Linny.

"Easy," I replied. "Your fort only has three walls. Where is the fourth one?"

"It does not need a fourth one," said Nicky.

"Yeah, that space is a big window," added my brother.

"Okay, where's the door?"

"Next to the window?" suggested Linny.

"Yeah, right. Okay, the girls win. I call it!" I cried.

"No way. We need a judge," said Nicky.

"How about me?" asked Linny. The boys laughed.

"Someone who won't take sides," said Nancy. "Maybe a grown-up."

"*Which* grown-up?" I asked. "I bet Daddy would take the boys' side and Elizabeth and Nannie would take our side."

"Then let's ask Elizabeth," said Hannie.

"No way!" cried her brother.

I stepped forward. I stepped all the way into the fort.

"What are you doing?" David Michael asked me.

I sighed. "Just thinking." I leaned against one of the walls.

Crrrreeeeeak.

"Karen!" screamed Hannie and Nancy and David Michael and Linny and Nicky. "Look out!"

Well, for heaven's sake. Do you know what happened then? The fort collapsed. It smashed onto the ground.

"Uh-oh," said Nancy.

But I said, "Hey! I think the girls won the bet!"

The boys looked at each other. "Yeah, I guess you did," said Linny.

"Wait a minute!" exclaimed David Michael. "What do you mean? Karen just wrecked our fort. That does not count!"

I looked at the mess I was standing in — broken boards and bent nails and dust rising around my ankles. The boys had said they were such good builders. They had spent more than a week building *this?* I smiled. Then I snickered. I covered my mouth with my hand. I *tried* not to laugh at the broken fort, but I could not help myself. I stared down at my feet. I could not look at Nancy and Hannie. I knew that if I did, they would laugh and then I would laugh and . . .

Too late. We were laughing anyway.

"What is so funny?" Nicky demanded.

"Nothing," I said. I ran back to my friends.

"Yeah, what is so funny?" said David Michael.

"Well . . . your busted-up old fort is. It's — " I stopped speaking when I saw David Michael's face. He looked awful. Like he wanted to cry but he was trying very hard not to. Linny and Nicky did not look much better.

I glanced at Nancy and Hannie. Now nobody was laughing.

It was my turn to feel awful. I pulled my friends away. We needed to have a conference. We had one in whispers. When we were finished I said to the boys, "Do you agree that our playhouse is better than your fort?"

David Michael stuffed his hands into the pockets of his jeans. "Yeah," he said. "I guess. Okay, it *is* better."

"Thank you," I replied. "Okay, the Three Musketeers have decided to call off the bet. You do not have to do our chores all summer."

"Karen?" interrupted Hannie. "How about

it if they do our chores until tomorrow? Just overnight?"

David Michael looked at Nicky and Linny. They nodded.

"One more thing," I went on. "We are a little bit tired of our playhouse, so you can use it until we leave tomorrow."

"Honest?" asked Nicky.

"Honest," I said.

"As long as you guys leave our garden alone," added Nancy. "And don't take down the curtains or anything."

"We won't!" cried David Michael. "Hey, thanks!" The boys ran off into the woods. "And tonight we will do anything you want!" called David Michael.

"That's a good thing," I said to my friends, "because tonight is the dance."

"Oh, my gosh! I almost forgot!" exclaimed Nancy.

"Luckily, I remembered to pack a dress," added Hannie.

"Maybe we should start getting ready right now," I said. "We want to look gigundoly beautiful. This will be a *grown-up* dance."

It was not even lunchtime, but Hannie and Nancy and I ran back to the cabin. We pawed through our suitcases and the bureau drawers. We took out our loveliest clothes. They were not quite as lovely as the clothes we would wear to church or temple, but they were nicer than what we were wearing. (The three of us were dressed in T-shirts, shorts, flop socks, and grubby running shoes. Also, our faces were dirty and our hair was hanging in our eyes.)

"We better shower first," I said. "And wash our hair."

So we did. "Are you girls feeling all right?" asked Jessi. (She was our baby-sitter that day.) "You are taking showers in the middle of the morning."

"We're fine," I told her.

After our showers we curled our hair. Then we spread our lovely dresses on one of the bottom bunk beds. We found clean underwear and clean party socks. I lent Nancy a yellow hair ribbon to match her dress, and I lent Hannie a blue hair ribbon to match her dress. *My* hair ribbon was made from red and purple shoelaces.

"Okay, let's get dressed," said Nancy.

"No, we should wait until after lunch," I said. "In case we spill. Plus, we can ask the boys to shine our shoes later."

When lunch was over, Hannie and Nancy and I got as dressed up as we could. Do you know what? I have a special bag that closes with a zipper. I keep makeup in it. Grown-up makeup. When Mommy or Elizabeth or Nannie is almost done with something like lipstick, they give the end to me and I keep it in that bag. I even have some perfume.

I waited until my friends and I were dressed. I waited until the boys had shined our shoes. Then I closed the door to the girls' dorm. I took out my makeup bag. I unfastened the zipper.

"Oooh," said Hannie and Nancy when they peeked inside. And Nancy asked me, "Do you know how to put on makeup?"

"Sure," I said. "I've seen Mommy do it hundreds of times."

I put lipstick and blusher and eye shadow and mascara on Hannie and Nancy and of course on me.

"Time for perfume!" I announced. "Look. This bottle is almost empty. We might as well use it up." Nancy and Hannie held out their hands. I poured perfume into them. Then I poured the rest into my hands. "Pat it all over your body," I said. "Especially on your neck and behind your ears. Oh, and on your feet, in case they smell."

When the Three Musketeers came out of the girls' dorm, Kristy was sitting on the porch. The boys were with her.

"Pee-yew! What stinks?" exclaimed David Michael.

"Girls?" Kristy raised her eyebrows at us.

It turned out we had put on a little too much perfume. We had to take showers again. Also, the dance was not formal. Kristy said it was casual. She said we did not even need makeup. Oh, well. Dressing up had been fun.

CHAPTER 21

Stacey

Friday Night

Tonight is the night of the dance.
I am really looking forward to it.
Everything here at Shadow Lake is
so much fun, Watson. Thank you for
a wonderful trip and a great vacation.

As you may have guessed, this was not *all* I had to say, but it was all I was going to put in Kristy's trip diary. I didn't want Watson reading about what else went on that night. He didn't need to know. I figured thanking him for the trip would be more comfortable for both of us. And for anyone else who might read this NOT private diary.

I am usually a little nervous before any dance. I guess most people are. After all, you don't know what might happen or who you might meet. Also, you want to look good, but I've discovered that the list of things that could go wrong with your appearance is endless. Particularly when makeup is involved.

The dance was going to begin after dinner, at eight o'clock. Around four that afternoon, Claudia nudged me. We were lying on the dock on towels, drying out after a long swim.

"Yeah?" I said. I shaded my eyes with my arm, and I rolled over to look at her. She was glistening with suntan lotion. (So was I.) And her hair was wet with lake water. (So was mine.)

"It's four o'clock," said Claudia.

"So?"

"The dance begins at eight."

"Yikes!" I cried. I sat up fast. "Boy, do we have a lot to do."

"Thank goodness we don't have to get too dressed up," I said.

"Really."

"Should we find Kristy and everybody?" I wondered.

"Oh, they'll come in when they're ready. Kristy'll probably come later. She's always saying she could get dressed up in five minutes flat. Not just dressed, dressed *up*," Claud said pointedly.

"Okay." We gathered up our towels and lotion and returned to the cabin. When we reached the girls' bedroom we found two surprises. One, everybody else was already there, even the little kids (little girls, that is). Two, the room reeked of . . . I wasn't sure what.

"What's that *smell*?" I couldn't help asking.

"Smells like cabbage," said Claud. "No, like cabbage and sewage."

"I was thinking," began Kristy, "that the smell was more like the one you get when you've just cleaned a fish and you're stuffing the head down the garbage disposal and something disgusting is already *in* the garbage disposal, like chicken skin. And the smells meet — "

"Gross me *out*!" cried Mary Anne. "Kristy,

don't you ever stop? You are always making me sick." Mary Anne turned to me. "She is *al*ways making me sick," she added.

"For your information," spoke up Karen haughtily, "that smell is *not* chicken heads or whatever you said. It is perfume. Lovely Lady perfume."

"It is?" said Mallory cautiously.

"Yes. Nancy and Hannie and I were wearing it but then you said the dance was a casualty, Kristy, not a formal, so we took showers."

"Casual," Kristy corrected her sister absentmindedly. "And I hope this doesn't mean the bathroom smells, too." She stuck her head in the door. "Aughh!" she shrieked. "Disgusting! The shower smells like perfume and soap and . . . and . . . something else."

"Lemon juice?" suggested Karen. "We rubbed lemons on our hands to help make the other smells go away."

"Yechh," said Kristy, and closed the door to the bathroom.

I looked at my watch. Fifteen minutes had passed, and I was no closer to being ready for the dance. The room was pandemonium, but I would simply have to do my best. Ignoring my friends and the squabbling (also the odor in the shower), I rinsed off the suntan lotion and washed my hair. Then I got dressed. Even though the dance was not "a casualty" I wanted to look my best.

Since we would be leaving for Stoneybrook the next morning, I gathered together all of my clothes (the clean ones) and spread them on a lower bunk. This created a mess, but I was just going to have to pack them into my suitcase soon, so I didn't mind.

While I was trying to decide on an outfit, Claudia wandered over and sat on the bed. (Actually, she sat on my Capri pants, but I wasn't going to wear them, so it didn't matter.) Claud glanced around the noisy room. When she was sure no one was paying attention to us, she said, "Have you figured out what to do about Sam?"

"About Sam?" I repeated.

"Yeah. Tonight? The dance? He'll be there, of course."

"I know. . . ."

"And?"

"Well . . . and I *don't* know."

"What if he asks you to dance?"

I frowned. Then I sighed. "Like I said, I don't know."

Claudia looked a little hurt. "Okay."

"Oh, Claud, I'm not — not holding anything *back* from you. Honest. It's just that I *have* been thinking about Sam, and I really *don't* know how to handle tonight. I'm sure there'll be something to handle, though."

"Probably you should just be polite. If he asks you to dance, then dance. Tonight's our last night. Whatever he says or does, go along with him."

"Even if he tells me I look 'raaaavishing, dahling'?"

Claud grinned. "Yup. Anyway, what's the worst that can happen?"

"He could make me look like a fool in front of everyone. He could dance like Frankenstein or something. That's exactly the kind of thing Sam would do. I think he actually *likes* making scenes."

"I guess you should just play it by ear."

"Hey, I know! Promise me something. If Sam and I are together and he starts to act like a *real* jerk, come rescue me."

"We ought to have a signal."

"Oh, good idea! I know. If I need rescuing, I'll blink my eyes at you. I just hope you'll be able to see me."

"I'll try to stay close by."

"Okay. Thanks, Claud. You are a true friend."

"Why is she a true friend?" asked Kristy from behind us.

"She's helping me with Sam," I replied.

Kristy made a face. "Sam's the one who needs help. Poor Stace. I'm sorry he's interested in you. And I apologize for the fact that Sam is my brother."

That evening we ate supper in a hurry. We ate in the cabin and the meal was sort of scattered, half of us eating while standing at counters, Karen and her friends eating out on the porch (where no one could smell them). Everybody was dressed and ready for the dance — and not terribly interested in eating.

We walked to the lodge in one big group, as if we were going there to eat dinner, but it was an hour later than usual, and when we reached the lodge we didn't go to the dining room. Instead we entered the ballroom, and found it decorated.

"It looks like a school dance," Mary Anne whispered to me.

And it did, balloons drifting down from the ceiling, paper decorations tacked to the walls, even a small band at one end of the room. However, unlike most of our school dances, the boys and girls did not divide themselves up on opposite sides of the room. Also, people began to dance right away. I saw Watson dancing with Kristy's mom, Charlie dancing with Emily, the Three Musketeers dancing as a group, and Jessi dancing rather unhappily with Daniel. What was going on with Jessi? I wondered. Mal would probably know. I turned around to look for her — and found myself facing Sam.

"Hi, Stacey," he said. "Would you like to dance?" Sam's voice was barely louder than a whisper. He was frowning slightly.

"Okay," I replied.

And at that second, the band ended a fast song and began playing a slow one. Sam opened his arms to me. Wordlessly, I fell into them and Sam guided me around the room. Once, I glimpsed Claudia. She raised her eyebrows at me and I smiled dreamily at her.

The next thing I knew, she had broken away from some guy I didn't know and was pushing her way toward me. What on earth — and then I realized. I had blinked my eyes.

Claudia was coming to rescue me. I shook my head (just slightly). I stared at her, eyes *wide* open. Finally, I waved to her over Sam's shoulder. Claud skidded to a stop. Her jaw dropped and her eyes widened. Then she blushed.

"SORRY!" she mouthed to me.

"THAT'S OKAY," I mouthed back.

Claud turned away.

I felt Sam's arms tighten around me. I laid my head on his shoulder. I closed my eyes (to

be on the safe side). And we drifted through the rest of the evening together. Has Sam liked me this way all along? I wondered. Have I liked him? Even without conversation, I knew the answer to both questions. Yes.

CHAPTER 22

Jessi

Friday Night

Ooh, the dance was just wonderful. Everybody had a wonderful time. The decorations and the food were wonderful. The band was wonderful. It was a wonderful last evening before the end of our wonderful vacation.

Jessi

Stacey wasn't the only one who couldn't tell the entire truth in Kristy's trip diary. Maybe you've guessed that I didn't tell the entire truth myself in my last diary entry. Actually, not only did I leave out some important information, but I sort of lied a little. The truth is that the dance, the band, the food, and the decorations were wonderful, but I did not have a wonderful time. Mostly, this was my fault.

"Jessi?" said Mallory before we left for the dance. "Are you okay? You seem a little, oh, nervous." We were in the girls' dorm. I was leaning into a mirror, putting on a pair of earrings, and Mal was standing behind me, looking over my shoulder.

"Who me?" I replied. "Nervous?" I dropped one of the earrings behind the bureau and had to crawl around on the floor to find it.

"Yeah, you," said Mal as I held up the earring and a dustball.

"Well, I guess a little. Yeah."

"But you like dances."

"I know. I've never been to one with Daniel, though."

Mal frowned. "I don't get it," she said.

"Mal, Daniel *likes* me," I explained. "And I

liked him, too, at first. But the boy I *really* like is Quint."

"And you think Daniel is going to . . . what?" Mal's voice trailed off.

"I think that at the dance tonight he's going to . . . profess his love for me."

"You *do?* Gosh," breathed Mallory, awed. "No boy has *ever*, um, professed his love for me. When Ben Hobart and I go to movies and to dances and stuff, we always, well, we always just watch the movies and dance. And talk, of course, but about things like what our brothers have done and why there should be movies that *adults* are not allowed to see."

"Daniel is older than Quint and Ben," I pointed out. "An entire *year* older."

"Whew," said Mal. "If things seem complicated *now*, imagine how they'll seem when we're sixteen and in high school."

I'm not sure why, exactly, I like certain people and dislike certain other people. I mean, it isn't as if all the people I dislike are axe murderers and every single person I do like is friendly and honest and smart and talented and . . . perfect. No, some people I really can't stand are all those good things. And my close friends are certainly not perfect. Kristy is bossy and Claudia's a slob and even Mal drives me crazy sometimes when she won't stop talking about how her parents are treating her like a baby.

This is why I can't say just how I knew I *really* liked Quint, and how I knew I just sort of liked Daniel. But I knew. I also knew that somehow, at the dance, I was going to have to let Daniel down. I was going to have to tell him my true feelings about Quint.

As we walked to the lodge after supper on Friday evening, I began rehearsing a speech. I planned to recite it to Daniel sometime that night. This is what I was going to say: "Daniel, I want you to know I've really enjoyed our time together here at Shadow Lake. The last week and a half have been a lot of fun. But I've decided that Quint, the other man in my life, means more to me than I'd realized. Daniel, I don't want to hurt you, but I just can't be your girlfriend. I hope you aren't too upset."

The speech seemed unfinished somehow, but I wasn't sure what to add to it. I prayed that something decent would spring to mind while I was giving the speech. A brilliant ad lib. Maybe even a witty one, so I could leave Daniel laughing.

"Jessi? Hey, Jessi!"

"Yeah?" I shook myself.

"Um, the lodge is *this* way," said Dawn, giving me a strange look.

"Oh," I replied, glancing around. We had almost reached the lodge and everyone else had just negotiated the right-hand turn off the path. But I had continued straight ahead.

I ran to catch up with the others and Mal laid her hand on my arm. "Jessi, get a grip!" she whispered loudly.

We entered the lodge, bypassed the dining room, and walked into . . . well, it's *called* the ballroom, but it does not look like my idea of a ballroom. I think of ballrooms as absolutely huge with tall, many-paned windows and a winding staircase down which party guests can make grand entrances. It starts out as just one staircase, then splits into two that meander down to the dance floor. At the windows are rich velvet curtains that are so heavy they don't even stir with a breeze, and hanging from the ceiling are gold and crystal chandeliers. Wait — gold and diamond chandeliers.

Now, I will admit that the ballroom at the lodge was beautifully decorated. Otherwise, it looked just like the dining room, without the tables and chairs. Dark wood, beams running overhead. Your basic big log cabin. And of course, no one was wearing gowns or powdered wigs. Pretty much, no one was even wearing dresses or neckties. Still, when my friends and I first stepped into the room, I caught my breath. I just love the aura of a dance, whether it's a ballet, a bunch of kindergartners in flower costumes, or a group of people ready to enjoy an evening together. I guess I love the concept of "dance."

"Jessi?" said a voice. This time it belonged to Claudia. "You're a million miles away." I nodded. I knew why. It was easier to daydream and to let my mind wander than to face Daniel and give my speech.

"Any particular reason?" she asked. She was grinning, as if she knew exactly what the reason was, but she wanted to hear me say it.

"I guess," I replied. "I — " And at that moment someone tapped me on the shoulder from behind. I turned around.

There stood Daniel.

"Jessi, you look lovely tonight," he said.

I guess I should have replied, "Thank you," but instead I said, "I do?" I mean, I was wearing a jean skirt, a yellow tank top, flop socks, and high-top sneakers.

"Yeah. You look gorgeous," Daniel said lightly.

Actually, I knew what he meant. Daniel was just wearing shorts, a polo shirt, and loafers, but he looked pretty gorgeous himself.

"Want to dance?" he asked.

"Sure," I replied. The band was playing oldies but goodies. Real oldies. They started off with "Chains of Love." Daniel led me to a spot smack in the middle of the dance floor. And as we danced, he kept smiling at me. I smiled back, but found I couldn't look directly into his eyes for more than a few seconds. Then my gaze would drift away, over his shoulder, and I'd realize I was watching Charlie whirl by with Emily Michelle in his arms, or the Three Musketeers, or Stacey and Sam. . . . *Stacey* and *Sam?* I did a double take. I must have seen — No, it was Stacey and Sam. They whirled by us again, and Stacey was actually smiling.

The band paused, then switched to a slow number, the second one of the evening. When the first one began, I had told Daniel I wanted to get some refreshments. But this time, he put his arms around me immediately. Uh-oh. Time to give my speech.

I leaned away from Daniel and looked up at him. "Daniel?" I began.

"Yeah?"

"You know, I'm leaving tomorrow. And I want you to know I've really enjoyed our time together here at Shadow Lake. The — "

"Me too."

I nodded. "Well, anyway, the last week and a half have been a lot of fun."

"Definitely."

"And — and, um." (I hadn't planned on my speech being interrupted.) "And — oh, yeah. I mean, *but* I've decided that Quint — remember, I told you about him — that Quint means more to me than I realized. Daniel, I don't want to hurt you, but . . ."

I stopped speaking when I realized Daniel was frowning slightly. He dropped his arms from around my waist. Oh, no. After all my planning I *had* hurt his feelings.

"Um, Jessi," said Daniel quietly, "I like you too, but I never meant for you to think I wanted to be your boyfriend. I just wanted to be your *friend*. I have a girlfriend back in Boston. Her name is Carol."

Whoa. I could feel my face burning. I was sure I had never, ever been more embarrassed. Oh, my lord, Daniel must think I'm the most conceited, self-centered—

But he was smiling. "I had a great time, too, Jessi, and I want to thank you for showing me how much fun dancing can be. In fact, I was thinking. How about one more lesson?"

I smiled back at him. "You got it," I said.

218

CHAPTER 23

Kristy

Saturday

Our vacation is over. How can it be over already? Vacations always go much too fast. People should be allowed to go on vacations in special time warps. Every day should feel like two days. Watson, I am being completely and sincerely sincere here. Shadow Lake is just the best place. I love the lake, I love the dock, I love the boats, I love the mystery, I love the lodge, I love Faith Pierson, I love our cabin, I even love the girls' dorm. The only thing I don't love is having to leave knowing we might not come back.

Kristy

All right, I know the last diary entry sounds a little desperate, but I meant absolutely every single over-written word of it. I prayed that if Watson had any doubts about deciding to accept the house — even after he read the diary — this entry would change his mind. It was my only hope. I was willing to risk sounding foolish.

Well, the dance ended, Friday ended, and Saturday arrived. Nobody woke up easily. Every one of us — my family, our friends — had stayed at the lodge until the band packed up their instruments and left, and the waitresses began to clear the refreshment tables. Here is something very gross: Stacey and Sam did not stop dancing until *after* the band had *left*. This means that for awhile the two of them were just dancing around the ballroom — alone — without music. (Oh, please. Give me a break. How could anyone get romantic with my *brother*?)

You should have heard Stacey after we returned from the dance. Well, actually, you should have seen her, since she wasn't saying anything. The girls were milling around in our bedroom, getting ready for bed. My friends and I were helping the Three Musketeers and Emily. Emily, by the way, had fallen asleep in

Watson's arms while we walked back to the cabin. Now she was sprawled on her bunk on her back, arms and legs flung out. We took off her clothes, put on her pajamas, and slipped her under the covers, and she never woke up.

Anyway, after Emily was in bed and the Three Musketeers were talking sleepily in theirs, my friends and I tiptoed onto the porch. We slumped into the wicker chairs and began whispering.

"Did you see me dancing with Andrew?" I asked. "He stood on my feet while I moved around. He said that way he wouldn't be able to *step* on my feet. I think we danced about five times."

In the dim porch light I saw Mary Anne smile. "He danced with me that way, too," she said. "Then I told him to dance with Emily Michelle, so he did, but they kept crashing into people's knees and falling down."

"I danced with two really nice boys," spoke up Mallory, "but we didn't tell each other our names." She was sitting under a bug-zapper, swathed in her mosquito netting, a can of Raid next to her. At least she had taken the netting off for the dance.

"I mostly danced with Daniel," said Jessi,

who didn't sound terribly excited about it. Not even very pleased.

Claud looked at her, frowning. "What's wrong?" she asked.

Jessi shrugged. She wasn't ready to tell us what had happened between her and Daniel. Not then. She told us several days later.

"Stace?" I said. (No answer.) "Yo, Stacey!"

"What?" She'd been staring up at the roof of the porch. Now she shifted her gaze to me, with a look that said she might or might not be aware of her surroundings. "Yeah?"

"Did you, um, have fun tonight?"

"Oh, yes." Stacey's voice was barely more than a whisper.

Gag, gag, gag, I thought, but I couldn't resist digging up just a *little* more information. "So, what exactly do you see in my brother?"

"Huh?"

"In *Sam!* What do you see in Sam?"

"Oh, he's gorgeous, Kristy. I don't know why it took me so long to notice. I mean, when I kind of liked him last year I thought he was cute and everything, but he's beyond cute. He truly is gorgeous. Maybe during the last year he blossomed. Like a flower."

I coughed, covering up a giggle, but the rest

of my friends were gazing solemnly at Stacey. (Later, Mary Anne said to me, "I recognize true love when I see it.")

"Girls?" called a quiet voice from inside the cabin.

"Yeah, Mom?" I replied.

"You better go to bed now," she said. "We won't be sleeping in tomorrow morning. We want to leave early and beat the traffic."

"Okay. 'Night, Mom."

The members of the BSC tiptoed back to the girls' dorm, checked on the little kids, then fell asleep.

Not surprisingly, Emily Michelle was the first one awake on Saturday morning. And she made sure I was the second one awake. I had been deeply involved in this dream about Stacey and Sam (they were getting married, but Sam was late to his own wedding because he was busy making goof calls from a pay phone in front of the church) when I felt a hand patting my face. "Morning! Morning! Morning!" a little voice said over and over.

I opened my eyes. Emily was sitting at the head of my bed. She removed a pacifier from her mouth and grinned at me.

I smiled back, but I took away the pacifier.

"Now where did you get that?" I asked her. "That's for emergencies, like when you start to cry in the middle of the supermarket."

Emily continued to smile.

"We might as well get up," I said. I peered at my watch, squinting my eyes. "Eight-thirty-five!" I exclaimed. "Oh, no! Yikes! Thanks for waking me up, Em."

I flew to Mom and Watson's room and rapped on their door. "It's after eight-thirty!" I called to them. Then I woke up everyone else. Half an hour later we were starting to load up the cars, and half an hour after that, we were eating a quick breakfast on the porch.

"I wish we didn't have to *leave*," said Karen pitifully.

"Me, too," agreed Andrew. "We have to say good-bye to Shadow Lake."

"How very, very sad," added Nancy dramatically.

Mallory swatted at a bug, missed it, and reached for the Raid.

"Don't spray that in here!" shrieked Dawn. "Not while we're eating!"

"And don't do *that* in here, either," I said to Stacey and Sam. They were sitting side by side, holding hands. They were also eating breakfast. (Note that Sam, who is right-handed, was eating left-handed, since his right hand was laced through Stacey's left hand. They could not even let go long enough to eat.)

Watson ignored my comment. "This has been a nice vacation," he said, setting aside a cantaloupe rind.

Of course, everyone began thanking him and Mom for it. Except me. I said, "Watson, have you made a decision about the cabin yet?"

Slowly Watson shook his head.

I was appalled. "You mean you don't want it? After all this?"

"No," he answered. "I just haven't made up my mind yet."

I let out a breath. "Oh," I said. Well, why hadn't he? "Please, *please* say yes to your aunt and uncle," I begged.

"I need to think about it a little more. Shadow Lake *is* fun, but now I see exactly how big a responsibility the cabin — and the boat and the dock — would be."

"I want to come back here and go swimming again," said Karen.

"I *still* want to build a fort in the woods," said David Michael.

"Boot!" cried Emily Michelle.

"Also, Shadow Lake's mystery isn't solved," added Dawn. "We can't just leave it hanging. That'll drive me crazy."

"This place is *so* romantic," whispered Stacey.

"I'll make a decision in a week," said Watson.

Not much later we were caught up in all the last-minute chores that must be done before leaving a house empty. We collected the garbage. We cleaned out the refrigerator.

"Hey, here's an ant!" cried Claudia.

"In the re*frig*erator?" asked my mother, horrified. "Is it alive?"

"Nope. Dead." Claud examined another shelf. She opened a plastic container. "Hey, here's a moldy yogurt. And the mold is red!"

Mom switched Claud to the job of cleaning the grill, and took over the refrigerator herself. At the same time she told the little kids to please check the bedrooms again and make sure they hadn't left anything behind. The kids grumbled, but soon we heard cries of, "Here's my rock collection! I almost forgot it!" (That was Nicky.) And, "Whoa, here's that bird's nest I found!" (Hannie.) And, "How did my bathing suit get under my bed?" (Karen.)

For awhile, the kids were busy running these items out to the cars, where Watson and Nannie tried to find places to pack them. I think that, if cars could bulge, ours would have.

Finally the last window had been closed and the last bureau drawer checked. Mom stepped onto the porch and locked the front door behind her. "I *know* we've left something behind," she said.

We piled into the cars. Watson had suggested that we return to Stoneybrook in the same cars in which we'd driven to Shadow Lake. This was a good idea, in theory, but right away, Sam insisted on riding in the same car with Stacey, and Andrew said he would *not* ride with Emily Michelle since she had gotten carsick before.

"I do not like people barfing in my lap," he said.

Neither did Stacey, which meant *she* couldn't ride in Emily's car. And the Three Musketeers refused to be split up. Getting the twenty of us divided into the three cars was like piecing together a living jigsaw puzzle, but finally we managed it to everyone's satisfaction.

We drove off, first through the woods, then by the big boat dock and the stores, and finally turning onto the highway.

Emily Michelle, who was now sitting next to me (I was equipped with several garbage bags), frowned and said, "Way go?" which means, "Where are we going?"

"We're going home," I told her.

"Mrow," said Boo-Boo from his carrying case.

"I have to go to the bathroom," said Linny.

And David Michael said, "Hey! I left my remote-control car in our fort!"

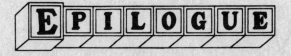

EPILOGUE

Kristy

We are in Stoneybrook again. I am glad to be here (home, sweet home) but I miss the lake and the cabin. There is something about being so close to nature. I just can't feel that way here. I try to pretend I'm in the woods, but then a car drives by, or the gears in a garbage truck begin to grind.

Anyway, we reached home safely. (Emily slept the entire way. She did not need the garbage bags, thank goodness.) Boy, did we have some fun reunions when our cars pulled into the driveway....

W hew. The front lawn of my house was as crowded as an airport. Here's who had turned up to welcome home their kids: Stacey's mom, Mr. and Mrs. Kishi, Dawn's mother and Mary Anne's father, Jessi's parents, Becca and Squirt, all the rest of the Pikes, Mr. and Mrs. Dawes, and Mr. and Mrs. Papadakis with Sari.

Nicky tried to open the door to the station wagon before Mom had even stopped the car. "Watch it!" I cried.

He held out for exactly three more seconds, then burst outside and into the arms of his mother and his father at the same time. A few moments later, *every*one was hugging. Emily Michelle, still sleepy from the car ride, was caught up in the emotion of the moment, and ran to the nearest pair of open arms (Mr. Ramsey's) for a hug. Then she glanced up, realized she was looking into the face of someone she barely knew, and burst into tears. (Luckily, Mr. Ramsey's feelings weren't hurt.)

Over the next few days, I finished getting the trip diary ready to present to Watson, and my friends wrote letters and postcards.

Dear Quint,

Shadow Lake was so much fun. We had a great time, but it would have been even better if you'd been there with us. In fact, I really wish you had been on the trip. You don't know how much I wish that.

Love and xxx ooo,

Jessi

Dear Jessi,

I MISS YOU! COME VISIT!

Yours till I see the salad dressing.

Quint (xxxxxooooo)

Dear Stephan,

I hope it's all right to call you that. I think about Annie and the mystery of Shadow Lake every day. I'm glad I met you. It's funny, but I feel as if I met Annie, too. Do you understand what I mean?

Sincerely,
Dawn

Dear Dawn,

If I can call you Dawn, you ought to be able to call me Stephan, no matter how old I am. Yes, I understand what you mean about Annie. I'll tell you a secret. Yesterday the oddest thing happened. I was working in the store and suddenly I was overwhelmed by a vision of Annie. She wanted to give me a message. She wanted me to know that one day somebody will find out what happened on the island, that I will know the truth. It's strange — I saw that image right after I received your postcard. Come back again soon, Dawn!

Yours,
Stephan

Dear Sir or Madame of the Bug-Off
Bug Spray Company,
　　I feel it is my duty as a Consumer to tell you that
your product doesn't really work too well. I used
Bug-Off when I went to this lake for two weeks
but I got seventy-eight mosquito bites anyway.
Maybe you should call your spray something else.
　　　　　　　　　　　Sincerely,
　　　　　　　　　　　Mallory Pike, age 11

Dear Ms. Pike,

　Thank you so much for your letter. Bug-Off appreciates all comments from consumers. Enclosed please find two coupons for fifty cents off of your next purchases of Bug-Off.

　　　　　　　　　　　Sincerely,

　　　Roger H. Humes
　　　　　　　　　　　Consumer Relations

One week after we returned from the lake, the trip diary was finished. I even typed it. I used our computer. I printed it out in red ink to make sure it would catch Watson's eye. Claudia and Mallory did some illustrations that we slipped among the diary pages, and then Mary Anne and I made a cover for the diary. We titled the diary: SUMMER TRIP — SHADOW LAKE. The book was *thick*. I was pretty proud of the finished product.

"How do you think I should present this to Watson?" I asked Mary Anne as we admired our work.

"Wrap it up," she replied. "Give it to him after dinner tonight."

And that is just what I did. When I handed it to him, I said, "Watson, this is for you from all of us. Sam and Charlie and David Michael and Emily and Andrew and Karen and I — plus our friends. I'll be honest. I'm giving this to you partly to say, 'See how much we love the cabin? We would like for it to stay in the family,' but mostly to say, 'We had a fantastic trip. Thank you for a wonderful vacation. We'll always remember it, and we want you to remember it, too!' "

Watson read the entire diary that evening. Then he sat at his desk and wrote this letter:

Kristy

Dear Aunt Faith,

My recent stay at the cabin in Shadow Lake was as enjoyable as my last stay there, when I was twelve. The children are in love with the cabin and the lake community, as are Elizabeth and her mother. I am writing to you to say that I would be honored if the cabin was willed to me.

Enclosed is a gift made for me by my daughter, Kristin Amanda (Kristy). I think you and Uncle Pierson will enjoy reading it — but I want it back when you are finished with it! It is a treasure.

Much love,
Watson

Watson called me his *daughter!* I think that's even better than being able to look forward to more vacations at the lake.

Before I went to bed that night I left a note for Watson on his pillow. It read:

Dear Watson,

Thank you! Thank you! Thank you! Thank you! Thank you!

Your daughter,
Kristy

About the Author

ANN M. MARTIN did *a lot* of baby-sitting when she was growing up in Princeton, New Jersey. She is a former editor of books for children, and was graduated from Smith College.

Ms. Martin lives in New York City with her cats, Mouse and Rosie. She likes ice cream and *I Love Lucy*; and she hates to cook.

Ann Martin's Apple Paperbacks include *Yours Turly, Shirley; Ten Kids, No Pets; With You and Without You; Bummer Summer*; and all the other books in the Baby-sitters Club series.

THE BABY-SITTERS CLUB®

by Ann M. Martin

More titles... ➤

The Baby-sitters Club titles continued...

Available wherever you buy books...or use this order form.

Scholastic Inc., P.O. Box 7502, 2931 E. McCarty Street, Jefferson City, MO 65102

Please send me the books I have checked above. I am enclosing $_____
(please add $2.00 to cover shipping and handling). Send check or money order - no
cash or C.O.D.s please.

Name _____

Address _____

City_____ State/Zip _____

Please allow four to six weeks for delivery. Offer good in the U.S. only. Sorry, mail orders are not
available to residents of Canada. Prices subject to change.

BSC1291

Enter THE BABY-SITTERS CLUB®

WIN A LOCKET CHARM BRACELET!

Super Special Trivia Giveaway

10 WINNERS

Take the Baby-sitters Club trivia challenge! Answer all the questions correctly and you have the chance to win a beautiful locket charm bracelet. Just fill in this entry page with the correct answers and return by November 30, 1992.

15 SECOND PRIZE WINNERS get Baby-sitters Club portable cassette players!
25 THIRD PRIZE WINNERS get Baby-sitters Club carry cassette players!

Fill in the blanks with the correct baby-sitter's name!

1. She has always lived on Bradford Court. _____
2. She is originally from New York City. _____
3. Baseball is her favorite sport. _____
4. She helped Jackie Rodowsky build a volcano for a science project. _____
5. She burns easily at the beach. _____
6. She has two pierced holes in each ear. _____
7. She would like to be an author. _____

Rules: Entries must be postmarked by November 30, 1992. Winners will be picked at random and notified by mail. No purchase necessary. Void where prohibited. Valid only in the U. S. and Canada. Taxes on prizes are the responsibility of the winners and their immediate families. Employees of Scholastic Inc.; its agencies, affiliates, subsidiaries; and their immediate families are not eligible. For a complete list of winners, send a self-addressed stamped envelope to: The Baby-sitters Club Super Special Trivia Giveaway, Winners List, at the address provided below.

Fill in this entry page and the coupon below or write the information on a 3" x 5" piece of paper and mail to: THE BABY-SITTERS CLUB SUPER SPECIAL TRIVIA GIVEAWAY, P.O. Box 7500, Jefferson City, MO 65102. Canadian residents send entries to: Iris Ferguson, Scholastic Inc., 123 Newkirk Road, Richmond Hill, Ontario, Canada L4C365.

Name_____ Age_____

Street_____

City_____ State_____ Zip_____

Where did you buy this *Baby-sitters Club* book?

❑ Bookstore   ❑ Drugstore   ❑ Supermarket   ❑ Library
❑ Book Club   ❑ Book Fair   ❑ Other_____(specify)   BSC192

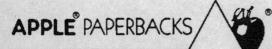

APPLE® PAPERBACKS

Pick an Apple and Polish Off Some Great Reading!

BEST-SELLING APPLE TITLES

☐ MT42975-2	**The Bullies and Me** Harriet Savitz	**$2.75**
☐ MT42709-1	**Christina's Ghost** Betty Ren Wright	**$2.75**
☐ MT41682-0	**Dear Dad, Love Laurie** Susan Beth Pfeffer	**$2.75**
☐ MT43461-6	**The Dollhouse Murders** Betty Ren Wright	**$2.75**
☐ MT42545-5	**Four Month Friend** Susan Clymer	**$2.75**
☐ MT43444-6	**Ghosts Beneath Our Feet** Betty Ren Wright	**$2.75**
☐ MT44351-8	**Help! I'm a Prisoner in the Library** Eth Clifford	**$2.75**
☐ MT43188-9	**The Latchkey Kids** Carol Anshaw	**$2.75**
☐ MT44567-7	**Leah's Song** Eth Clifford	**$2.75**
☐ MT43618-X	**Me and Katie (The Pest)** Ann M. Martin	**$2.75**
☐ MT41529-8	**My Sister, The Creep** Candice F. Ransom	**$2.75**
☐ MT42883-7	**Sixth Grade Can Really Kill You** Barthe DeClements	**$2.75**
☐ MT40409-1	**Sixth Grade Secrets** Louis Sachar	**$2.75**
☐ MT42882-9	**Sixth Grade Sleepover** Eve Bunting	**$2.75**
☐ MT41732-0	**Too Many Murphys** Colleen O'Shaughnessy McKenna	**$2.75**
☐ MT42326-6	**Veronica the Show-Off** Nancy K. Robinson	**$2.75**